"I hate you!" China cried, fighting her desire...

Ben's dark brows lifted. "And you can't bear my touch. Quite a transformation. I might believe you, except I've tasted your response, your mouth, your soft white skin, China. They're branded on my memory." His voice was husky, and her face burned with humiliation.

"Ben, I...you...." Her voice trailed off as she saw the restrained violence on his lips.

"I should have taken your beautiful white body when I had the chance," he said darkly, his eyes flaring with raw desire.

"You wouldn't have got the chance," she retorted heatedly.

Ben smiled thinly. "You couldn't have stopped me—you wanted me, darling, almost as much as I wanted you." His gaze was openly insolent, as though he could see through the silk dress to her body beneath.

PATRICIA LAKE
is also the author of these

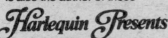

Harlequin Presents

465—UNTAMED WITCH
501—PERFECT PASSION
521—WIPE AWAY THE TEARS

PATRICIA LAKE

heartless love

Harlequin Books

TORONTO • NEW YORK • LOS ANGELES • LONDON
AMSTERDAM • PARIS • SYDNEY • HAMBURG
STOCKHOLM • ATHENS • TOKYO • MILAN

Harlequin Presents first edition October 1982
ISBN 0-373-10538-X

Original hardcover edition published in 1982
by Mills & Boon Limited

CHAPTER ONE

IT was a beautiful late-summer afternoon, but China felt worried as she strolled back to Clare's flat, far too preoccupied to appreciate the clear blue sky and the cool, bracing air. She had strolled along the river bank to buy the local newspaper at the village shop, hoping against hope that there would be a job that suited her advertised, but as usual she was disappointed.

The useless newspaper was stuck in her coat pocket now, and she trudged along with her head down, moodily kicking up the first autumn leaves with the toes of her leather boots. It wasn't only a job she needed, in fact that was one of her smaller problems, she thought wryly, as she climbed over the rickety wooden gate and back on to the road. Her most pressing need was accommodation, because in a couple of weeks' time when Clare got married, she would be literally out on the street. Goodness knows how I manage to get myself into these ridiculous situations, she thought miserably, suddenly feeling her self-confidence, shaky at the best of times, slipping away into nothing.

She turned the corner of the narrow lane and strolled towards the main road. She had been foolish to give up her job in Italy, she supposed, but she had been left with very little choice.

In the cold English afternoon air, she yet again let her mind stray back to the time she had spent in Rome. There had been such good times, lovely, sunny times. I *was* happy there, she told herself fiercely, wondering why she had to cling to her memories of happiness so desperately.

When she had left the convent orphanage at the age of eighteen, it had been so easy to get a job. She had answered an advertisement in a well-known magazine, for a nanny to two Italian children. It had been a surprise, receiving the letter that asked her to attend an interview at a London, hotel. Both Signor and Signora Cencelli had been there, the atmosphere had been friendly and informal, and within two dizzying weeks, China had found herself in Rome, in charge of Franco, aged six, and Giulia, aged four—beautiful dark-eyed children whom she had fallen in love with immediately.

The two years spent with the Cencellis had flown by, while China grew to love their huge modern apartment near the city, and she had travelled widely throughout Europe with the family, picking up the Italian language easily.

It had all been so perfect; they had welcomed her as one of their family, something she had never known before, and she had felt needed and even loved. Adele Cencelli was only a couple of years older than China and they had soon become close friends. That was what hurt most, the loss of Adele's friendship, that and leaving the children.

Even now, so many months later, China felt a shiver of disgust when she thought about her last few weeks in Italy. It had all been so ugly and so bitter, because she had never doubted the happiness of the Cencellis' marriage not once, and she had never noticed how Signor Cencelli sometimes looked at her. She supposed that was the naïvety she was so often accused of.

When Adele went into hospital for a small operation, China and Signor Cencelli had been alone in the evenings, and she had begun to feel uncomfortable, so uncomfortable that she had started to take dinner in her room. Then one evening he had made a rather obvious but totally unexpected pass at her. China had felt physically sick, slapped his face hard and locked herself in her room, shocked and terribly shaken.

After her obvious and disgusted rejection, he had turned nasty, his pride badly damaged, and had made her life a misery—anger, cruel remarks; it had been a dreadful time for her. It made her feel a little sick even now.

The whole unsavoury business had placed her in a very difficult position. She had wanted to resign, to leave immediately, but she was loath to hurt Adele, who would need her more than ever now that she was ill. She need not have worried, she now thought bitterly, because Signor Cencelli had brought the situation to a head one evening soon after Adele was released from hospital.

China had been lying on the balcony of the apartment after tucking Giulia and Franco up in bed, trying to summon up the energy to change for dinner, when Signor Cencelli had appeared in front of her. She had jumped to her feet, hating what she had seen in his dark face, anxious to escape, but he had cornered her, trying to kiss her, his eyes insolent, his hot, slimy hands reaching for her. China had fought like a wildcat, but only Adele's shocked and disbelieving gasp behind them had brought Signor Cencelli to his senses.

Adele had been hurt and very angry, and a horrifying row had ensued. China had packed her belongings and left the following day, shocked, numb and very sad.

That had been over two months ago, and she had come to Clare, her best friend, her only close friend

from the orphanage. Clare had been so good, so kind,
that China would never be able to repay her. She
had insisted that China should stay with her for as
long as she wanted, and had brought her out of herself again, helping her to forget what had happened
in Rome.

That whole period of her life was best forgotten,
she knew, but over and over again her mind ran
through it. Signor Cencelli had somehow shattered
her young, romantic illusions about men; she mis-
trusted them now, even though some tiny, secret part
of her mind still felt sure that they could not all be
bad. But she was frightened of love and what it could
do to a person, leaving them at the mercy of their
emotions. It was definitely not for her, and what she
would never understand about the Cencellis was
why. Adele was so beautiful and so loving, the perfect wife. *Why?*

So deep was she in thought that she did not notice
that she had reached the main road. A second later,
the loud blaring of a car horn, accompanied by a
terrifying screech of brakes, broke into her reverie
and she glanced up in bewilderment, her blue eyes
wide and expressionless, to find herself only inches
away from a huge grey car that would have surely
run her down.

The driver was sliding from the car and China
prepared an apology in her head. It was her fault,
she had not been looking where she was going and it
was a miracle that she had not been killed or at least
badly hurt.

As this realisation sank in she began to tremble
with shock and reaction. The driver strode towards
her and she looked up at him. He was tall and dark
and very, very angry.

'You bloody stupid little fool!' he snapped harshly.

'Don't you ever look where you're going?'

China frowned, startled by his fury, and raised her calm eyes to look into his face. It was closed with dark anger, thin and hard-boned with a high-bridged nose and hooded amber eyes that lanced through her from beneath frowning black brows.

She did not answer him, her apology sticking in her throat in the face of all his anger. Her seemingly calm silence, however, seemed to infuriate him further and he reached out and grasped her shoulder roughly, his strong fingers digging into her flesh, shaking her until the pale silver curtain of her hair fell over her face and a retaliatory spark inside her ignited her temper at such unreasonable behaviour. But before she could speak, the man grated, 'What in hell's name is the matter with you? Dammit, I came within an inch or two of killing you!'

China was angry too now. She lifted her head and flicked back her heavy swathe of hair, pulling free from the stranger's grasp.

'I assumed that those ridiculous questions were rhetorical. Don't you think you're overreacting a little?' she asked levelly, although her blue eyes were flashing with anger, born of shock.

The man stared at her, his peculiar golden eyes totally unreadable.

'This is a country road,' China continued coolly, 'and I've no doubt you were driving much too fast.' She cast a disparaging glance over his shoulder at the sleek grey car—a Porsche, she recognised from an article she had read recently in a Sunday newspaper. It was a car made for speed and for one unreasonable moment she felt that it proved her case. The man smiled faintly, but his apparent amusement did not reach his eyes which were still blank and cold. He was still staring at her, and China tilted up

her delicate chin in defiance and stared right back.
If he thought he could intimidate her then he could
think again!

She supposed he was attractive in an arrogant,
overbearing way. He was certainly wealthy, the car
and the beautifully-tailored suit he wore gave that
away.

'Is that an accusation?' the man asked, his low
voice suddenly quite calm and flat. Deceptively
calm, China thought uneasily. It had an edge to it
that was infinitely more frightening than his anger.

At that moment she was suddenly tired of this
ridiculous confrontation. She had been in the wrong
and would have apologised immediately if he had
not acted so arrogantly. But it had gone too far, he
was obviously a totally unreasonable man, and she
felt sure that she had the right to save what was left
of her pride.

She lifted her eyes and glanced at him boldly.

'Interpret it any way you wish,' she said coldly,
inwardly baulking at what she saw in his icy amber
eyes. 'Now, if you'll excuse me. . . .' She wanted to
get away from him, and the sooner the better. He
still held her shoulder, but there was no violence in
his touch and she shrugged free easily and turned
away.

'Oh no, you don't!' He moved fast and silently
and China found him standing in front of her again,
within a split second. He was very close to her,
almost touching, and she could still feel the anger
inside him and it frightened her because it reminded
her too much of what had happened in Italy. It was
too soon for her to forget. Fear lit her eyes, a flash of
iridescent blue in her pale face. It was as if these two
separate incidents had merged into one, for some
crazy reason, and she stood before Signor Cencelli.

The stranger, who was still standing near to her, reached out to detain her again and she whirled away from him in panic. His hand on her arm seemed to trap her and she pushed at it, unconsciously aiming blows at his broad chest with her free hand.

She sensed his surprise and a certain stillness in him as his anger dissolved.

'Take your hand off me!' she hissed at him, her face alight with fear, her eyes brilliant with anger.

He stared at her with shrewd curious eyes but ignored her furious request. The whole situation had shifted slightly and as China stared into his unfathomable golden eyes, for what seemed like ages, the strange moment of confusion passed and she remembered who he was. He was not Signor Cencelli and she had no reason to fear him, apart from his possessive grip on her arm. I must be cracking up, she thought to herself.

As she quietened, she looked at the hand on her arm. It was strong and tanned and long-fingered.

The man watched her carefully, then released her. China felt confused and tired and she knew for certain that she had made a dreadful fool of herself. She did not even dare to look at him in case he was laughing at her.

'Are you ill?' the man asked quietly. There was an irritated edge to his voice, coupled with a seemingly exaggerated patience that grated along her nerve endings.

She looked up into his face then, carefully schooling her features into calmness. He did not seem to be laughing at her and there was something about his dark face that caused a slight pain deep inside her.

'Are you always so patronising?' she demanded icily.

His beautifully-moulded mouth twitched a little as though she had said something funny. He *was* laughing at her, she thought furiously, unable to stop the rush of hot tears into her eyes..

'I had no idea I was being patronising,' the man replied in an expressionless voice.

'It must come very easily to you, then,' China said quickly. Then, 'Are you waiting for an apology?' She knew that she was being childish but could not help herself. She felt raw and vulnerable and there was something about this man that sparked antagonism in her. Obviously the reverse was also true, because she saw his mouth tighten at her insolent question.

'It would not be unwarranted,' he drawled coolly, 'but I expect nothing from a demented child like you.'

It was a deliberate insult and she longed to slap his face, but some instinctive inner knowledge of him held her back. She felt absolutely certain that in any displays of temper or violence, she would fare much worse than him. So, instead, she smiled carefully, showing her perfect white teeth.

'You really are a brute,' she said quietly but very clearly. 'I only hope that I never have the misfortune to meet you again.'

If she expected an angry response she was disappointed, because quite unexpectedly, the man threw back his dark, saturnine head and laughed out loud.

She stared at him for a moment wondering, as she thought about this strange and tension-filled encounter, who was the most insane, herself or him. He was shaking his head. 'You're absolutely crazy,' he murmured, still obviously amused.

China glared at him, hating him at that moment, more than she had ever hated anybody in all her young life. It seemed so easy for him to make her feel childish and silly.

'I have no intention of spending my afternoon standing here and being insulted by you,' she said stiffly, unaware of how contemptuous she sounded.

The golden eyes flashed at her. 'Am I detaining you?' he asked flatly and rather insultingly, his glance sliding over the slender length of her body in slow, almost insolent appraisal. China felt her face flushing under this leisurely scrutiny and her temper rising again. She felt inexplicably shabby and untidy in her short fur jacket and old green velvet trousers tucked into her long leather boots, and for some crazy, ridiculous reason she wished that she was looking her best.

This strange and unreasonable longing for him to like her was the final straw and turning on her heel, she strode away without a further word. She did not look back at him, unable to bear his obvious amusement, and as she walked past the sleek, powerful car she had to fight the almost overpowering urge to give it a good kick.

I've obviously underestimated my own talent to amuse people, she thought furiously, as moments later, still without turning her head, she heard the car's engine purring into life. Then with a low roar, the car and the infuriating stranger were gone, and even as China breathed a heartfelt sigh of relief, there was still some small traitorous part of her that regretted such a nasty encounter.

She pulled herself together with a visible effort, admonishing herself for being so stupid. The best thing to do would be to forget, as quickly as possible, this disastrous afternoon. But even as she walked briskly back to Clare's flat, she could not help wondering about the man in the Porsche—far too much for her own peace of mind.

She reached the flat in double-quick time, walking faster than usual because she still felt a little angry. It was a large Victorian house that had been divided into flats, five years previously. Clare's flat was on the top floor, large and spacious, and China had asked about taking it over when Clare got married, but she had been unlucky. Clare's lease ran out exactly two weeks after her wedding day and the landlady wanted the flat for her own daughter, who was recently divorced.

China pushed open the huge front door of the house with a sigh and ran nimbly up the long flights of stairs to the bright yellow door with Clare's name on it. She hunted in her pocket for the key and let herself in.

'Clare! I'm back!' she shouted, shrugging out of her jacket and hanging it up behind the door.

'Any luck?' Her friend appeared from the kitchen, holding a mixing bowl, her dark hair pushed into an untidy bun on the back of her head, smiling as usual.

China shook her head, smiling back. 'Not today, I'm afraid,' she said lightly, unable to stop her heart sinking at her own casual words.

Clare must have noticed something, because her face became serious and sympathetic.

'You'll find something, love, I'm sure,' she said reassuringly.

China managed a smile. 'I know, I just wish it didn't take so long. Shall I help?' she asked, changing the subject quickly. Inexplicably, she felt close to tears and needed something to take her mind off her problems. Any more of Clare's kindness and she would probably sink into a mire of tears and self-pity.

Clare cast her a swift look of understanding. 'Did you get the broccoli?'

'Oh no, damn, I forgot!' China clapped her hand to her forehead in dismay. 'I'll go now—I'm sorry, it completely slipped my mind.' She moved towards the door to retrieve her coat.

'It doesn't matter. Actually, Mrs Collins brought up a huge bag of sprouts from her husband's allotment just after you left, so we can use those for dinner,' Clare laughed. 'Hey, don't worry, I prefer sprouts anyway,' she added, seeing China's stricken face.

China laughed then, and they strolled into the kitchen together. There was a wonderful aroma issuing from the oven, and China's nose twitched.

'Beef Wellington,' Clare said in answer to her unspoken question.

'What shall I do?' China tied an apron around her slender waist as she asked.

'The potatoes?' Clare grimaced, not liking to ask.

'Right.' China set to work, collecting the vegetable peeler and a huge bag of potatoes from the cupboard. 'How many for dinner?'

Clare shrugged resignedly. 'Now you're asking! I'm not really sure—either four or five.' And as China shot her a curious glance, she added, 'It's Paul, he's bringing a good friend of his tonight and *maybe* his good friend's brother, who may or may not have to be back in London this evening.'

The way she said it made China laugh. Clare was so perfectly equipped to deal with Paul's vagueness, a vagueness that was so much a part of his lovable character. They had met a year before at art college, both on the same fashion course, and Clare often related the story of how they had nearly missed each other on their first date because Paul had got the arrangements wrong. Clare had been waiting at the cinema and had seen Paul on a bus that had stopped at a red light. He had been on his way to another theatre and she had jumped on the bus and caught him just in time. Clare's upbringing in the orphanage, exactly the same as China's, had made her practical and efficient, the perfect foil for Paul.

Looking at her friend now, China envied her in the nicest possible way. Clare had love and security, something China had wanted for as long as she could remember. Oh dear, I'm slipping back into my self-pitying mood, she thought wryly, and attacked the potatoes in front of her with renewed vigour.

Once all the food was prepared, they set the table in the huge dining room. Clare had bought some flowers that morning and China carefully created a delicate centrepiece for the table. The result was elegant and satisfying, and the table looked very attractive as she went to take a quick shower before changing.

Ten minutes later, she was drying her pale silver hair with Clare's hairdryer, and wondering what to wear. She was also wondering why she had not mentioned her humiliating encounter with the arrogant stranger on the road. His lean, angry face rose before her eyes. He was undoubtedly a very attractive man—wealthy, with a hard air of success and breeding about him, and although she did not want to, she found herself wondering about him and wishing that she had found out more about him. Too late. She felt sure she would never see him again. Good riddance, she told herself just a little too fiercely, as she switched off the dryer and concentrated on her face.

She never wore much make-up, and tonight was no exception. She had far too many other things on her mind to worry about her face, so after applying a couple of coats of mascara to her long, silky lashes, and outlining her lips with a colourless lip lustre, she strolled over to the wardrobe and flicked through her clothes, wondering what to wear. To her own irritation she still could not get the stranger's face out of her mind and she found herself remembering things about him, tiny irrelevant details that she had barely noticed when she had been with him – his unselfconscious grace, his strange, angry eyes. I don't know what's the matter with me, she thought wildly; I didn't even like him.

Forcing her thoughts to blot him out, she finally chose her dress for the evening, a delicately-printed Indian cotton dress in pale colours, threaded with silver that glinted and glistened in the light as she moved.

She slipped into it, pleased that it looked good, complementing her pale hair and accentuating her beautiful eyes.

Fastening a thin silver chain around her neck, on which hung her favourite pendant—the only thing she had of her mother's, delicately engraved and containing a small faded photograph of the woman she had never known—and slipping her feet into high-heeled sandals, she was ready, and went back into the kitchen to check the food.

Everything seemed to be under control—Clare was an extremely competent cook. China was just checking the potatoes when the intercom buzzed. It was Paul. She pressed the button that opened the main door of the house and told him to come up, then she called Clare.

'Could you be a love and give him and whoever he's got with him a drink? I'll be ready in five minutes,' Clare called from her bedroom, sounding rather flustered.

'Okay—don't rush, I'll keep them occupied,' China shouted back, trying to soothe her friend.

There was a knock on the front door and she went to open it. Paul stood outside with another young man that China did not know.

She smiled. 'Hello, Paul, do come in.'

'Hello, love, how are you?' He moved towards her and kissed her cheek.

China kissed him back. She was very fond of Paul. He was warm and friendly and generous, and although he was a vague personality, she had it on good authority from Clare that he was well on the way to the top of his chosen profession.

She looked at him now, taking in his open, handsome face, his neat fair hair and his casually smart clothes. He handed her two bottles of wine.

'I thought these might help,' he laughed. 'I had no idea what we'd be eating, so I brought both.'

China took the bottles, feeling her earlier depression disappearing as she smiled at him.

'Lovely,' she said enthusiastically. 'Do they need to be chilled?'

A discreet cough behind Paul broke into their pleasant conversation and brought his head round.

'James, my dear fellow, I'm sorry—I should have introduced you.' He cast an apologetic look at China, who was having difficulty keeping her face straight. It was typical of Paul to forget all about the friend he had brought to dinner.

'You must be Clare—Paul has told me so much about you, and I can see there was no exaggeration.' The young man stepped forward and shook China's hand, flashing her a brilliant and charming smile.

China found it infectious and smiled back at him.

'I'm afraid I'm not Clare,' she told him gently.

'And who are you?'

'Oh dear, it's all my fault,' Paul broke in, sounding confused. 'I'd better start again. China, this is James Galloway. James, this is China Harmon, Clare's flatmate and best friend.'

James' blue eyes were alight with amusement as they solemnly shook hands again.

'Forgive me, Miss Harmon, although I have to say that I'm profoundly grateful that you're not Clare.' He was obviously flirting with her, but China found that she did not mind.

'Please call me China,' she said with a smile, gently rescuing her hand which he seemed loath to let go.

'Only on condition that you call me James,' he replied, quite seriously, even though his eyes were still glinting with amusement.

'James it is. Now do come into the sitting room, both of you, and I'll fix drinks.' She flashed Paul a friendly but exasperated glance and he lifted his shoulders resignedly as they strolled into the softly-lit room.

'Where's Clare?' he asked as she took the men's coats.

'Just getting changed, she'll be here in a moment.' She hung up the coats in the hall and popped the white wine into the refrigerator, and was pouring out drinks for everyone when Clare appeared, looking stunning in a mauve-coloured silk dress, her newly washed hair looped into an attractive chignon.

The introductions started again, and Paul was teased unmercifully over his disastrous handling of the introduction of China and James.

On returning to the sitting room from the kitchen where she had been checking the vegetables, China took her opportunity to study James Galloway. She guessed that he was in his late twenties and she found his thin, animated face very attractive. He was chatting to Clare and Paul and she found it easy to gauge his personality.

He had thick mid-brown hair, styled back from his face, and even features, with a thin high-bridged nose that reminded her a little of. . . . Good grief! I must put the man in the Porsche out of my mind, she thought, purposefully turning her attention back to James. His mouth seemed a little sullen, but perhaps she was wrong, too over-critical.

She could also admire his taste in clothes. He was wearing dark corduroy trousers in brown with a matching waistcoat and a pale, off-white shirt that was obviously made of silk. All in all he looked good, young, self-assured and attractive, and she had the feeling that she would like him if she ever got to know him.

She had been sitting in the corner of the room on one of the fashionable cane and chintz chairs that Clare had bought cheap at a warehouse sale in preparation for her wedding, and even as she finished her careful examination of James, he looked round and saw her sitting alone. He smiled, letting his eyes run over her in undisguised admiration, and stood up, walking over to her.

'All alone?' he asked lightly.

China smiled at him and shook her head. 'No, I like to listen,' she answered honestly.

'How long have you known Clare?' His eyes lingered on her face and she suddenly felt rather happy. James Galloway would be very easy to handle, uncomplicated, and perhaps that was just what she needed.

'Since I was six and she was seven,' she answered pertly, casting her friend an affectionate glance.

'Ah, childhood friends—how lucky you are, China. The only friend I have from my childhood is my brother.' He sounded so sad that China laughed.

'You poor thing,' she mocked gently. 'What happened to all your friends?'

James shrugged, his face alive with self-amusement. 'It's terribly sad, isn't it? All alone in the world with only my brother for companionship.' His voice was dramatic. 'No, actually, we moved about the country such a lot when I was a boy, and not just this country either, that it wasn't until I got to university that I actually settled anywhere long enough to make proper friends. Not that I'm complaining,' he finished, pulling a funny face.

'What did your father do?' China asked curiously. She was always very interested in other people's families, probably because she'd never had one of her own. She knew that she would have travelled twenty-four hours a day for all of her life, if it meant that she had been part of a loving, caring family.

'He was a diplomat,' James replied with a grimace.

'Still, it must have been nice to travel so much,' said China, unable to shake off a slight feeling of wistfulness.

James looked at her seriously, picking up a certain sadness in her voice.

'I guess so. And your father, what did he do?'

China lowered her head. 'I never knew him,' she said evenly. 'But I believe he was a doctor.'

James took both of her hands in an instinctive gesture of comfort and sympathy.

'I'm so sorry, China. I can be such an insensitive brute sometimes, rabbiting on about my family.' He sounded so sincere that China felt quite hurt inside, for a second, and angry with herself for being so silly.

She lifted her head and flashed him a dazzling smile. 'Please don't apologise—I love hearing about other people's families. Tell me about your brother. Is he the man that Clare thought might be coming here for dinner tonight?'

The moment of awkwardness was over, and she saw the relief in James' eyes that he had not hurt her.

'Yes, that's Ben. He has a house here, a huge rambling place that he's been doing some repairs to over the past couple of weeks. Unfortunately he had an urgent phone call from London and had to drive down there this afternoon.'

'Ben Galloway—that name sounds familiar somehow,' China mused aloud.

'It should do, he's a big property tycoon, quite famous, actually,' James told her, with just a hint of pride in his voice.

'Of course! I think I read something about him in the papers last week.'

'More than likely,' James said drily. 'Ben's hot news—he has quite a playboy image—it's all rubbish, though, believe me.'

'You're very fond of him,' China said with a smile.

'Yes,' James answered simply. At that moment China spotted Clare, signalling to her from the kitchen. She got to her feet gracefully.

'Excuse me,' she said to James, 'I must give Clare a hand with dinner.'

In the kitchen everything was ready and China helped Clare by draining vegetables and warming plates. They were having a rich game soup for a starter, and China poured it into a lovely old tureen that had belonged to Paul's grandmother.

'You seem to be getting on very well with James,' Clare remarked with a speculative smile.

'He's very attractive,' China replied vaguely.

'Yes, he is,' Clare agreed. 'And he can't seem to take his eyes off you.'

China laughed, wondering if that was true. She had not noticed, and a secret smile curved her soft mouth.

Over dinner, as the food was well complimented, the wine flowed freely and the atmosphere was warm and friendly, Paul suddenly asked,

'Any luck with a job and a place to live yet, China?'

She shook her head. 'I'm afraid not. You know what the employment situation is like at the moment, and as for accommodation. ... I expect something will turn up, though,' she finished brightly.

'I'm sure it will,' Paul murmured encouragingly.

James, who had been listening to this exchange, suddenly said with a huge smile, 'Well, if you're only looking for a job and somewhere to live, I think I might have the answer.'

There was a sudden silence around the table and China stared at him fixedly, hardly understanding what he had said.

'What ... what do you mean?'

'I mean, if you need a job with live-in accommodation, then I can help you,' he repeated slowly, with a faint air of secrecy.

'Oh, do tell, James!' Clare broke in, her voice mingled excitement and exasperation.

'I don't know. ... I do enjoy being the centre of attention, you know,' James teased. Then, glancing at China's sweet, hopeful and worried face, he said, 'Ben has recently bought a house near here—you may know it, Aspenmere Hall. And he's looking for a housekeeper to live in. I told him this afternoon that I'd try to find a local woman while he's in London. Frankly, China, the job is yours if you want it.'

CHAPTER TWO

THE very next day at eleven o'clock precisely, James' car pulled up outside the flat. China, bright with excitement, was waiting for him and had reached the front door of the house and flung it open before he had time to ring the bell.

She had spent an almost sleepless night, only drifting into a light slumber at dawn, her mind whirling around as she wondered about the job and the house, fervently praying to herself that her problems would be over. But even though she had only managed to get a couple of hours' sleep, she was radiant with excitement, almost glowing with energy and enthusiasm as she confronted James.

'Good morning, beautiful,' he said with a smile, his openly admiring eyes taking in the attractive picture she made in black velvet trousers that hugged her slender hips and tucked into knee-length black leather boots and a short sheepskin coat.

'Hello, James. Can we go?' she asked breathlessly and so quickly that her words tripped over themselves, having to restrain herself from tugging at his sleeve.

'Aren't you going to invite me in for coffee?' he teased in reply, staring into the brilliance of her eyes.

China fought to control her disappointment at such a delay. 'Of course ... come up,' she said, managing a smile.

James looked at her for a moment, then laughed. Her expression was so very easy to read.

'I was only joking,' he explained gently. 'I'm not in the least bit thirsty.'

China stuck out her tongue at him. 'Pig!' she laughed, happy again.

'Shall we go?' he asked, offering her his arm.

'It's just that I can hardly wait to see the house,' she explained as he slid into the low car beside her.

'I understand how you must be feeling, but I've been thinking about the whole situation and wondering if you realise exactly what you'll be taking on if you take the job. It's a big barn of a place, you know, and you'll be there all alone when Ben is away. . . .' He paused, seeing the worried expression in her eyes. 'I don't mean to dampen your enthusiasm, love, I just want you to realise that it's not the only job in the world, and if there's anything about it that you don't like, I'm sure I could help you find something else—Oh hell! I'm making an awful mess of this,' he finished miserably.

China squeezed his arm lightly, careful not to interfere with his driving.

'I appreciate what you're saying, James, honestly I do, and I know that I'm getting ridiculously carried away about your brother's house, but I can't help it. Ever since I moved in with Clare, I've been looking for something, and disappointments day after day are pretty wearing,' she explained slowly. 'You see, I don't know many people, so there isn't really anybody I can ask for help. I'm so glad I met you, though.'

'So am I,' James replied, taking his eyes off the road for a second to flash her a smile. 'I'm sure we're going to be great friends.'

There was silence for a few moments because China did not know how to answer his remark and she was thinking about what he had said. All of a sudden, a frown pleated her smooth, pale brow and she turned to him in agitation.

'Does your brother know about me? Did you ring him last night?'

'I tried, but I couldn't get through. But I did offer to find him a housekeeper and he had no objections,' James said cheerfully.

China sighed. It all seemed too easy, especially after months of fruitless searching.

'But what if he doesn't like me?' she fretted, feeling terribly worried suddenly.

'There's not much chance of that,' James replied, sounding perfectly serious and very relaxed. It was not exactly the answer she had hoped for, but James seemed to know what he was doing, so she decided to leave it entirely in his hands. Worrying was useless, after all.

Fifteen minutes later, the car turned off the quiet main road, through stone pillared gates on which sat huge stone eagles, chipped and worn with age, and down a gravelled tree-lined drive. China sat up in her seat and looked around with interest at the wild, neglected gardens to both sides of the drive, until the Hall came into view.

It seemed enormous, and her indrawn breath communicated some of her shock to James.

'Not bad, eh?' he laughed.

'I only hope I haven't bitten off more than I can chew,' China said, breathlessly.

'As I said before, you don't have to take the job. It is pretty daunting, I must admit, but it's really quite small as these country houses go, you know.'

Looking at the building objectively now, China realised that he was telling the truth. It really wasn't such a big house, in fact it looked fairly compact.

'I was comparing it to Clare's flat, I suppose,'

she said to herself, not realising that she was thinking aloud until she heard James laugh.

The car pulled to a halt and he turned in his seat to look at her.

'Let's go and look, shall we?' China nodded enthusiastically and jumped out of the car.

The huge, solid front door was painted white. James opened it and they stepped inside. The whole place had a deserted air about it, China thought with a shiver, as she wandered through the large entrance hall, even though it was all newly-decorated and smelled faintly of polish. Ben Galloway obviously had very good taste, and she let her hands wander over the old and warmly-coloured wood panels.

'How long has your brother lived here?' she asked curiously, turning around to find James watching her with warm, amused eyes.

'He hasn't moved in yet. He only bought the place a couple of months ago and since then he's been having it renovated and redecorated. It's all finished now, as you can see, so I expect he'll be moving here pretty soon,' James said vaguely.

That explained the deserted air of the house.

'Where does he live now?' she asked, still looking around with wide eyes.

'He has a house in London—he's been living there and abroad for the past three years.' James sounded bored, and China did not question him further, but allowed him to show her round the house.

It was not as large as she had expected, but it was still very impressive and had been modernised without any destruction of its original charm.

The huge drawing-room retained its beamed ceiling and the walls were painted a rich brown colour that contrasted beautifully with the thick, pale carpet and leather chairs. Enormous, exotic plants, some as tall as small trees, decorated the room, along with various sculptures, paintings and objets d'art. The whole room had an air of wealth and serenity, the effect essentially masculine. It was quite, quite beautiful.

Together, China and James walked through the whole house, and China was open in her admiration. No expense had been spared, it seemed, in refurbishing the old building.

The study was oak-panelled and lined with bookshelves. The floor was of polished wood, partially covered with a breathtakingly beautiful Chinese carpet, and the open fire was laid, needing only a match to set it alight.

There were so many rooms that China was soon dazed, unable to take everything in, only receiving an overall impression of tasteful beauty. One of the things that surprised her most, although she really did not know why, was the swimming pool. A large glass conservatory built on to the back of the house had been converted into a heated, indoor swimming pool, surrounded by lush, verdant plants and bright cane furniture, with a row of brightly-painted changing rooms against one wall. The water was calm and blue and inviting.

'It's amazing!' she gasped, almost to herself, trying to imagine swimming in this tropical paradise when the winter snow was falling outside.

James smiled. 'Ben certainly knows how to live,' he said, and China wondered for a moment at the expression in his voice and in his eyes. But a second later it was gone as he took her hand.

'Now I'll show you the servants' quarters,' he joked, and led her back into the house.

A self-contained flat, completely separate from the

rest of the house, had been created on the ground floor. There was a sitting-room with a large window overlooking the wild gardens, and a carved fireplace, a bedroom with a large brass bed, antique wardrobes and a private telephone, and an adjoining bathroom with a rich royal blue suite. There was also another room that had a convertible couch-cum-bed in it.

To China it was like a palace and she instinctively knew that she wanted to live there.

'It's lovely!' she breathed, her eyes brilliant as she looked at James. 'I want the job—and thank you so much for offering it to me. I'll work hard and I won't let you down, I promise.'

James was staring at her as though he could not drag his eyes away.

'You could never let me down,' he said softly.

'You know what I mean!' China laughed, refusing to take him seriously.

He walked over to the window and gazed out towards the distant hills. It was dark for the middle of the day and the heavy, scudding clouds promised rain.

'It's very isolated here, won't you mind?'

'Are you trying to put me off?' China asked, punching his shoulder lightly.

'No, of course not. I just want you to be sure,' he answered seriously, turning back to look at her, waiting for her answer.

'I won't mind living here alone, in fact I'll positively enjoy it,' China said firmly. 'I've lived with people not of my own choosing all my life and I think it will be heavenly, *heavenly* to have my life to myself and live here,' and she twirled round delightedly.

James shrugged. 'Well, if you're sure. . . .'

'I am. Now, is the job mine? Do put me out of my misery,' she begged.

'On one condition,' said James, with a slightly mischievous smile, and China raised her eyebrows.

'What?'

'That you have dinner with me tonight.' He sounded very serious and she exploded with laughter.

'Fool! I'd love to have dinner with you tonight.'

With that sorted out, they went on to discuss the details of the job. James rang his brother from the study, and China could not bear to listen just in case Ben Galloway refused her the job at the last minute. So instead she went to inspect the kitchen which she would have use of for herself as well as her employer. It was marvellous—not that she expected anything different after seeing over the rest of the house. Completely modernised, it contained every imaginable labour-saving device, including some that were new to her.

It would be a joy to wash and cook in a kitchen like this, she thought, remembering the depressingly old-fashioned, workhouse type kitchens at the orphanage.

She stood in the middle of the kitchen, closed her eyes tight and crossed her fingers. Please, please let Ben Galloway give me the job, she prayed, and was still standing there when James found her. She heard him enter the room and spun round to face him, her blue eyes huge in her suddenly pale face. At that moment, it was the most important thing in her life, in the world. She *must* get this job!

James was silent for a moment, and she could not bear that silence.

'Well?' she prompted desperately, in a small voice.

'The job's yours,' he said, with a smile breaking

over his face. She had not realised that she had been holding her breath until it was released at his words.

'Oh, James, thank you!' Almost unaware of her actions, she hugged him, weak with happiness and relief.

James hugged her back and China knew as they stood together that she had found a true friend in him. It was a good feeling and one that she would cherish for a long time to come.

'What did he say?' she asked when they finally released each other.

'Well ... he said he would have preferred a married couple with the husband seeing to the gardens and general repairs, but I told him that you were very reliable, keen, that you'd do a good job and that he wouldn't find anybody better. He agreed and asked if you could cook. I said you could. Can you?'

'Yes. I'm quite a good cook, actually—or so I've been told,' China replied honestly. 'It sounds as though he wasn't too keen to give me the job,' she added, rather wistfully.

'Only because he'd thought of getting a married couple in,' James said reassuringly. 'Anyway, you've got the job, so what does it matter?'

'You're right, it doesn't matter at all,' she replied, her happiness returning.

'What he wanted was somebody reliable. You are reliable and I told him so. He was perfectly happy—honestly!'

'Will he be coming here to interview me, or whatever?' China questioned, wondering what she would wear to impress James' rich brother.

'No. Unfortunately, he's tied up with business at the moment and he's flying out to Italy tomorrow, so he told me to give you the keys. You can move in whenever you like—I'll help, of course.' He handed her a slip of paper. 'That's the salary he's offering. He said that if you're not satisfied with it, then he'll sort it out with you when he gets back.'

China unfolded the scrap of paper, gasping as she saw the figure scribbled on it. She looked up at James with wide, saucer eyes.

'It . . . it's far too much,' she stammered, wondering if this was a wonderful dream. She would probably wake up any moment to find herself in Clare's flat, jobless.

James laughed. 'It doesn't seem excessive to me,' he said drily, 'and I'm quite sure Ben will make you work for it.'

It was obviously a fairly normal wage as far as he was concerned, and China hoped that he did not find her gauche.

'Anything else?' she asked, feeling quite dazed by such good fortune.

'Mm—oh yes, there's a Mrs Stephenson who comes in most mornings. She does all the heavy cleaning, so you don't have to bother with that. And this,' he handed her what seemed like a huge wad of banknotes, 'this is a month's salary in advance and some extra money for stocking the house with food and any other expenses you might incur.'

'Good grief!' China sat down suddenly, her legs giving up on her. 'I can't believe this is happening,' she whispered, dropping the money from shaking fingers on to the tiled table.

'And I think that's all,' James finished, tapping his chin thoughtfully and sounding very businesslike. All these crazy, wonderful arrangements seemed so very ordinary and everyday to him and she could hardly believe it. All her problems had been solved within twenty-four hours, it was better than she could ever have imagined.

'Any other business can be sorted out when Ben gets back. Can you think of anything else?'

James was still talking and China forced herself out of her daydream to pay attention.

'I can't think straight at all,' she admitted wryly. 'I can't thank you enough, James, for all you've done.'

'That's what friends are for,' he told her, with a gentle smile. 'And I don't know about you, but I'm starving—shall we go and find some lunch?'

They lunched by the river at an old inn with a roaring log fire. They both had steak and because she had not been able to manage any breakfast, being so nervous and excited, China found herself ravenous. She wanted to pay for the meal as a kind of thank-you for all James' help, but he would not hear of it, turning the whole thing into a joke.

'What sort of man would I be if I asked a lady out to lunch and then let her pay?' he teased as he asked for the bill, and China had to capitulate.

James dropped her back at Clare's flat two hours later, refusing to come in, saying that he had a business appointment, and it was only as the car pulled off that China realised that she had no idea what business he was in. Ever since they had met, she had been solely concerned with herself and his brother. How dreadfully selfish I can be, she thought sadly, remembering the faintly bored note in his voice as he had answered her endless questions about his brother. I shall insist that he talk about himself all night, she decided, thinking about their dinner date that evening. I do hope he's not offended.

Clare was ecstatic when she heard the good news. China told her as soon as she got in, finding her friend working at her sewing machine in the front room.

'Oh, China, I'm so glad for you! I felt sort of responsible that you couldn't take on this flat, but now everything has turned out perfectly,' she said excitedly, jumping to her feet to hug China, uncaring that the material she was working on fell to the floor.

They spent the afternoon drinking endless cups of coffee and sorting out the arrangements for China moving out. There was no reason why she should not move into Aspenmere Hall within the week, and she started sifting through her belongings, immediately. She did not have much to move, in fact it would probably only take her one journey in her battered old Mini.

'One of the few advantages of living a travelling life,' she told Clare with a smile.

She dressed carefully for dinner with James, wearing a simply cut black crêpe dress, adorned with a small diamond pin that had been a Christmas present from Adele Cencelli. She also took particular care with her make-up, wearing a little more than usual, especially on her eyes. She had set her hair and it fell in long soft waves around her small pointed face and slender shoulders.

She was definitely looking her best, and James' eyes told her that she looked beautiful when he picked her up at exactly eight o'clock.

Over a delicious meal at a wildly expensive restaurant, she found out that he was an accountant, just starting up in his own business. She wondered, without asking, why he did not work with his brother, but she could sense the rivalry in James; he wanted to make it on his own, and she could not blame him for that.

She also learned that he lived in a flat in a new,

luxury building just outside the town. He was on his way to the top and he was cool, clever and ambitious. China had no doubt that he would become as well-known as his brother.

But despite that rather ruthless ambition he was easy and amusing company and she found herself laughing a good deal during the evening.

He was curious to know when she would be moving into Aspenmere Hall, offering to help her with the move. She told him that she would be in by the end of the week and politely refused his offer of help. It would not be a big move and she rather fancied doing it by herself; it was about time she asserted her independence.

'I'm twenty years old,' she told him. 'And it's time I stood on my own two feet for a change, instead of relying on other people's kindness.'

'So old, so worldly wise,' James teased in reply, stroking a gentle finger down her cheek. He seemed to understand that it was something she felt she had to do herself and did not push his offer of assistance.

China could not remember laughing so much as she did that evening, and she told James so as he dropped her off outside Clare's flat. She asked him in for coffee, but he refused, explaining that he had a very early call the following morning. He kissed her forehead gently and promised to call in at Aspenmere Hall as soon as she moved in—in fact he would probably telephone her at the flat before she left, and he would definitely see her at the wedding, he told her.

As soon as she got inside, after waving to him as he drove off into the night, she felt exhausted. Lack of sleep the night before, coupled with everything that had happened that day, seemed to suddenly drain her. There was no sign of Clare, so she went straight to bed, falling deeply asleep as soon as her head hit the pillow.

China had decided to move into Ben Galloway's house on the day Clare got married, exactly a week after she got the job. It was a quiet register office wedding, and James was the best man.

Clare looked radiant and quite beautiful in a white voile suit, and China felt tears gathering in her eyes as Clare and Paul made their vows. They seemed so happy together and the ceremony was so very touching, she could not help crying.

There was a small wedding breakfast at Paul's house immediately afterwards, and China spent most of the time chatting to James. She asked him whether or not he knew when his brother would be back at Aspenmere Hall, but James told her that Ben was still in Italy and he had no idea of his plans.

When the party was over, Clare and Paul set off to the airport to catch their plane to Mexico where they would spend their honeymoon, and China was among the knot of people who crowded on to the pavement to wave them off.

Then they were gone, and everybody dispersed and made their way to various cars.

'Today's the big day, then,' James said lightly when they were the only two left.

'Yes, I'm moving in this afternoon,' China told him, unable to keep the excitement out of her voice.

'Sure you don't want any help?' James glanced at his watch as he asked.

'No, you're a very busy man these days, but thanks anyway,' she smiled.

'How about dinner tonight?'

She thought for a moment. 'Yes, that would be lovely.'

A long black saloon car pulled up alongside them as she spoke and the driver leaned out of the window to greet James. He turned to China with a sweet, regretful smile.

'Did you bring your car?'

'It's over there.' She pointed across the road.

'I have to go. Eight o'clock tonight—I'll call for you. Do you like dogs?'

'Yes, but. . . .' She had no time to finish her puzzled question, because he kissed her cheek hurriedly and jumped into the black car. Then he was gone, leaving China staring after him, wondering if he was mad. She shook her head, it was useless to try and work out what he had been talking about, and strolled over to her car.

The flat was empty except for her own pile of belongings in the sitting-room. Faintly depressing. She made herself a cup of coffee after changing out of her grey flowered silk suit into serviceable denim jeans and a cornflower blue jumper, and sat on the window ledge, feeling sad.

Paul had collected all Clare's things in a hired van, the night before, and driven them to his house. China looked around the room; she had been happy here and would miss Clare dreadfully. She lit a cigarette and idly smoked it while she finished her coffee, then she rinsed her cup and purposefully got her things together. It was the start of a new life for her, no time to be maudlin.

As it happened, with careful packing she found that she could fit everything into the Mini in one go, so taking a last look around the flat, saying goodbye and making sure that nothing important had been left behind, she slammed the door shut for the last time and handed in the keys at the flat downstairs.

As she neared Aspenmere Hall her sadness dissolved a little, to be replaced with anticipation. She knew instinctively that taking this job had been a wise move.

She parked her Mini at the back of the house and let herself in the side door. It was much nearer to her rooms and it would be infinitely easier to carry her things in that way.

It took her an hour to unpack her clothes into the beautiful old wardrobes and the chest of drawers, her first task after carrying all her possessions in from the car. It gave her a sense of belonging to see her clothes hung up and various ornaments and trinkets dotted around the rooms. Her one prize possession, a small abstract oil painting by a well-known Italian artist, she hung on the wall opposite her bed, so that she could see it every morning when she woke up.

She placed her cosmetics in the lovely blue bathroom, then laid the fire in her sitting-room. The light was fading, the afternoon dark and windy, so she drew the heavy velvet curtains, lit the fire and switched on all the lamps in the room.

It was warm and cosy and beautiful, her own private place to live. She made some coffee when everything was done, and sat by the fire drinking it, listening to the wind howling through the trees outside.

A feeling of warmth and security filled her and she must have dozed off, because she was woken by the clanging of the front door bell, and glancing at her watch, she saw with horror that it was eight o'clock. That would be James, ready to take her out to dinner, and she had not even changed.

She pushed back her heavy swathe of hair and jumped to her feet as the bell rang again, rushing out to open the door. James stood outside with a basket in one hand and a paper carrier bag in the other.

'Oh, James, I'm so sorry! I must have fallen asleep, and I haven't even washed and changed yet,' she explained quickly. Then she saw the rain, his hair was dark with it. 'Come in, I didn't know it was raining.' She stood back to let him in and he stepped inside, smiling at her. 'What have you got there?' she asked curiously, pointing to the things he was carrying.

'Wait and see,' he replied mysteriously, and as she opened her mouth to protest, he added, 'Don't say another word. You haven't given me a chance to open my mouth since I arrived.' He looked and sounded so stern, yet his eyes were bright with amusement and China burst out laughing.

'I'm sorry—I just felt so flustered when I woke up and it was so late. Come through.'

They strolled into her cosy sitting-room and James looked around with interest at the personal touches she had added, while China stoked up the fire and threw on some more logs.

'It looks good in here,' he remarked, putting down the large basket and the bag, and shrugging out of his wet coat.

She took the wet garment from him. 'Thank you. Would you like a coffee?' And before he could answer, she added, 'Oh, do tell me what's in those bags, I can't stand it!'

James took her gently by the shoulders and sat her down. 'Sit down, be quiet and I'll tell you,' he ordered laughingly. China did as she was told. 'I thought that you might be too tired to go out for dinner tonight, so in there'—he pointed to the carrier bag—'is everything that I'll need to whip up a de-licious meal for two, to say nothing of wine and dessert. And in here,' he knelt down by the wicker basket and began to undo the leather buckles, 'is your housewarming present.' He opened the lid and China looked inside, where a very small, very adorable puppy sat looking up at her with huge brown eyes.

'James, he's beautiful!' she breathed, picking up the little black dog, who proceeded to lick her chin thoroughly. She smiled at James. 'So that's what you meant this morning.'

'Indeed. He'll keep you from being lonely and I think he'll be a good guard dog when you're here alone. I have it on good authority that he's house-trained, so you needn't worry about that either,' James told her, obviously very pleased with himself.

'What shall I call him?' China wondered, as she stroked the small black head.

'How about Fortune?' James suggested. 'As an omen for your new life.'

'Fortune.' China tried it out and the puppy pricked up its ears and licked her nose enthusiastically. 'He seems to like it,' she giggled. 'So Fortune it is.'

James watched her playing with the little dog, a curious expression lighting his eyes. China caught that expression as she glanced up at him and instinctively knew that he wanted her. She turned away from that thought, recoiling from it fearfully. She wanted James as a friend, nothing more. She had thought he understood that.

'Did you say you wanted some coffee?' she asked, her voice suddenly small and rather frightened as she sought for something to say.

'No, I don't think so.' That strange, hungry look was gone as quickly as it had come and everything was back to normal again.

'I think I'll start preparing the meal,' he decided.

'Do you want any help?' James shook his head. 'You look after Fortune and introduce him to his new home.'

'I didn't know you could cook,' China teased, as he picked up the bag of provisions.

'I'm a man of many, mostly hidden, talents,' came the witty retort as he walked through to the kitchen.

There was no time to change, so China washed, then brushed out her long silver hair, with Fortune following her everywhere, looking up at her with huge, loving eyes. A relationship seemed to have sprung up between them already, and China felt glad. She had never had a pet before. She would have to buy him a collar, a name-tag and a lead. It would be good fun.

James' meal was a great success. As he had said, he was a very good cook. They had lamb chops in a rich savoury sauce and vegetables followed by chocolate gateau—not baked by him, he admitted—cheese and fruit. It was relaxed and pleasant, and China, however hard she looked, saw no signs in his face of the emotion she had caught in that split second before the meal. She hoped it had been her imagination.

The next morning she woke early, wondering where she was for a second, and felt a tiny dart of happiness pierce through her as she remembered, looking around the bedroom, her eyes coming to rest on her painting. It was a dull rainy day and looking out of the window, she saw that the trees were rapidly losing their leaves now as autumn approached.

She struggled out of bed, singing to herself. Even the dull weather could not dampen her happiness to be in this beautiful house. She fed Fortune in the kitchen and made some coffee, wondering if Mrs Stephenson would be in today. She would shower and dress, then explore every room in the house again. Then after lunch she could stock up with food for the return of the unknown Ben Galloway.

As she sipped her coffee she wondered what he was like. Was he perhaps an older, wealthier edition of James? That would be nice, although she could not bank on him being like James. I do hope that we'll get on with each other, she thought worriedly. I'll make him like me and I'll do such a good job that he'll be satisfied and maybe even glad to have me as his housekeeper.

On this positive note, she finished her coffee and strolled into her bathroom to take a shower before dressing. She switched on the hot tap and nothing happened, apart from a loud, metallic rumbling from the pipes. She switched the tap off, left it for a few seconds, then tried again. Nothing. Damn, she thought, hardly an auspicious start to the day. She then tried the hot tap on the hand basin, with the same result—not a drop of water. She could not understand it, because the cold taps were working perfectly, but obviously, on a day as cool as this, a cold shower was out of the question.

Then the idea came to her that she could try one of the other bathrooms in the house. Nobody would ever know. She grabbed some towels and her shampoo, and making sure that Fortune was firmly shut in the kitchen she ran up the impressive main stairway, a slight, graceful figure in her lace nightdress.

The bedroom she found herself in was obviously Ben Galloway's. It was very masculine and very luxurious, with dark red walls and a huge bed covered with dark red satin sheets. Even the windows were shaded with deep wine-coloured wooden blinds, and China laughed aloud, wondering what sort of man would have a bedroom like this.

She could not resist sitting down on the bed and the sheets were cool, smooth and sensual beneath her fingers. Did he have lovers? she wondered, staring at the aggressive framed prints on the walls. Undoubtedly, with a bed such as the one she was sitting on.

Fitted wardrobes and beautifully polished furniture—her eyes rested on everything in the room as she tried to assess the personality of her new employer. It was quite an effort to bring her mind back to her shower, and she jumped off the bed and strolled into the adjoining bathroom.

This too was decorated in a rich dark red, with long mirrors and masculine toiletries scattering the polished surfaces.

'Obviously a man with a passion for red,' she told herself aloud, catching sight of herself in one of the huge, shiny mirrors. She looked almost ridiculously feminine in this aggressively masculine room. Her hair was wild and tousled, her blue eyes looked huge and very bright in her small face and her curved, slender body looked seductive in its pale lace. She looked like a stranger. How peculiar that a room can do all this, she thought curiously.

She reached for the shower tap and miracle of miracles, it worked! The steaming water was pouring out of the gold taps and she quickly stripped off her nightdress—she had spent far too much time daydreaming, already—and stepped into the deliciously hot shower.

She had just shampooed her hair and was giving it a final rinse when to her horror, horror that froze her where she stood, she heard somebody entering the bedroom. She closed her eyes for a second, then she remembered Mrs Stephenson and let out her breath on a long sigh of relief, which was completely destroyed a moment later as she heard distinctly masculine whistling issuing from the bedroom and getting nearer to the bathroom by the second.

It must be James, she thought worriedly, cursing herself for not locking the door, praying that he would not enter the bathroom. That would be too embarrassing.

'I'm in the bathroom, James, I'll be out in a moment,' she called loudly, deciding to give him a warning.

The whistling stopped immediately, and before China knew what was happening the glass door to the shower was flung open and a low, angry voice that China remembered very well demanded, 'What the hell are you doing in my shower?'

CHAPTER THREE

It was the worst moment of her life, and her whole body stiffened as she stared into the face of the man in the Porsche who had almost knocked her over a week or so before. She could not have answered his angry, demanding question for the world, and was too shocked to even reach for a towel to cover her nakedness.

'Lost for words?' he queried in a very soft voice, and China flushed hotly.

His hard golden eyes moved over her in slow appraisal and, too stunned to do anything else, she looked blindly into his lean, arrogant face. Those eyes were hypnotic, and to her everlasting shame, she could feel her body responding to his intimate glance. Her breasts ached heavily, the nipples hardening as he stared at her, his glance so intent it was almost a physical caress.

His stormy eyes returned to her face then, pinning her mercilessly, not allowing her to look away, the steaming water still falling around her gleaming body.

His mouth twisted. 'Very pretty! You're certainly a change from my brother's usual choice in women.' His voice was flat, cold, and at that instant, China came to her senses, as though released from a spell that had held her paralysed for long moments. She grabbed one of the huge red towels from the rail near the shower and quickly wrapped it around herself, her face still burning with shame and embarrassment.

When he had appeared she had thought, for some insane reason, that he might be a burglar, but as soon as he had said 'my brother', the awful truth had dawned on her. He was Ben Galloway, her new employer. It should have been anybody in the world but him, she thought desperately.

'A little late for a show of modesty, I would have thought,' Ben Galloway remarked, his narrowed eyes cynical.

China lowered her head, humiliation welling up inside her at his cruel remark. She did not know what to say to him, her throat was closed and she wished with all her heart that the ground beneath her feet, in point of fact a thick cream carpet, would open up and swallow her whole. She twisted back in one supple graceful movement and turned off the taps, then turned to face him again.

She licked her lips nervously, knowing that she had to say something to him. He was standing near to her, his body perfectly still, his eyes still narrowed on her face. And he was waiting for an explanation.

'I . . . I'm sorry. . . .' she began nervously, acutely embarrassed and feeling more uncomfortable by the second. Cold water from her long pale hair was dripping down the heated skin of her back, making her shiver even though her body felt as though it was on fire.

She let her glance skitter over his face for a second. It was completely enigmatic, cold and closed except for his eyes, and they were piercingly alive and focused on her face. She wondered inconsequentially if he was enjoying this. He probably was. She tried again.

'I. . . .'

'I know, you're sorry, but it's a little late for that too, isn't it, sweetheart?' he enquired derisively.

'Brother James downstairs preparing breakfast, is he?'

For a second, the implications of his words did not sink in, but when they did, China felt her anger flashing through her like a raging fire, and before she had managed to control or question her actions, she had reached up, uncaring that the towel slipped down to reveal one taut breast, and delivered Ben Galloway a stinging slap across the face.

She did not have the strength to hurt him, of course, but she had a moment of triumph at the surprise she saw mirrored in his cold eyes. It was shortlived, because he reached out and grabbed her wrist, his long, tanned fingers tightening cruelly on her fragile bones, giving her no opportunity to cover herself. If she moved her other hand then the towel would probably slip off altogether.

She remembered then, as she stood there completely at his mercy, their last disastrous encounter. She had wanted to hit him then, but had drawn back, frightened of his reponse, sensing that she would fare worst. She now knew that for a fact, and regretted her impulsive behaviour.

She tried to free her wrist from his imprisoning fingers, but it was useless, and she did not dare to move much because of the towel.

'Let me go, you swine!' she hissed, angrier with him than she had ever been in her life.

'So that you can hit me again? I don't think so. And besides, you look very fetching in that towel,' he drawled insolently, resting his golden gaze on her bared breast.

China's anger left her with the realisation that she was fighting a losing battle. She did not know this man and if she was not very careful he would probably humiliate her again.

'If you have to use this kind of brute force to get your kicks, then please look as much as you like,' she said in a tight, icy little voice, hoping that it would have the desired effect and he would let her go so that she could run from him, to hide and try to forget this dreadful scene that she felt sure would haunt many of her nightmares for weeks to come.

Unfortunately, her cutting remark did not have the desired effect. Ben Galloway merely smiled, a twisting of his firm mouth, with no answering amusement in his cold eyes as he said pleasantly— far too pleasantly,

'What a nasty little mind you have! Is that what my brother finds so appealing in you, I wonder?'

He was being deliberately insulting, but he suddenly let her go, quickly, abruptly, as though the touch of her skin against his hand disgusted him.

'Get dressed,' he said coldly, glancing at her scantily-clad body with vague distaste. He reached into his pocket and pulled out a cigarette case and placing a cigarette between his lips, lit it with graceful ease. From beneath her lashes China looked at him assessingly, as she waited for him to leave the bathroom. He looked like a gypsy today, a far cry from the suave man in the expensive suit that she remembered. He wore tight, faded denim jeans that clung to his flat stomach and lean hips, and a dark cotton shirt that hung open revealing a hard, muscular, tanned chest, liberally scattered with short dark hair. He had obviously been expecting to use the shower himself.

He looked tired and unshaven, with faint shadows beneath his strangely-coloured eyes. She looked at his face. Framed by thick over-long dark hair, it was lean and strong with prominent cheekbones and a well-defined jaw. Just to look at him caused a slight pain around her heart that she could not understand.

He had not moved, but stood smoking, expelling thin streams of smoke from his beautifully-moulded mouth, watching her watching him.

'Would you mind?' she asked cuttingly, flashing him a brilliantly angry look.

The dark brows lifted in faint amusement. 'If you insist. Rather pointless, though, don't you think?' He let his amber eyes wander over her once more, leaving her in no doubt of his meaning before turning and strolling unhurriedly from the room.

As soon as he had gone China sank on to the side of the bath, covering her face with her hands. How terribly embarrassing! This was hardly how she had imagined her first meeting with her new employer. She had recognised him immediately, of course, and that had been her first dreadful shock—that this cold, arrogant brute could be James' brother. It was unbelievable, and it did not bode well for the future. Had he recognised her? she wondered. It would be surprising if he hadn't, unless he made a habit of driving dangerously, she thought sourly. On the other hand, if he had recognised her, why hadn't he mentioned it?

She got to her feet slowly, finding that she was trembling from head to toe with reaction. It was more than obvious that he would not want her working for him. She would not think about it.

She dried herself quickly and slid into her lacy nightdress, which she had no doubt would be damning in his eyes. Oh, why didn't I at least bring my dressing gown? she moaned silently. But it was too late to think of what she might have done.

Taking a deep breath, still visibly shaking, she opened the bathroom door and walked into Ben

Galloway's bedroom with her head held high. Her pride, after all, was the only thing she had left.

He was standing with his back to the window, frowning, and as he saw her, he straightened and stubbed out the cigarette he was still holding. China stared at him, hoping that she had managed to erase the fear inside her from her face.

His eyes flicked over her, slim and tense as she stood before him wrapped in pale, seductive lace. His mouth compressed tightly as he looked over at the bed, and following his gaze, China saw with dismay the clear imprint of her body, where she had been sitting on it, realising at that moment just what he thought. He assumed that she had been sleeping with James, in his bed.

'Mr Galloway——' she began, in an effort to explain.

'You do know who I am, then?' he cut in harshly.

She nodded. 'If you'll only let me explain——'

He crushed her with one cold glance. 'Explanations seem singularly unnecessary,' he said darkly. 'I want you out, sweetheart, now. Understand? Get dressed and leave.' He was hard and unyielding.

China sighed and tried again. 'Mr Galloway, James gave. . . .' He took a step towards her and she shrank back against the wall. His powerful body seemed menacing, but although he was furiously angry, she could see that he was completely in control of himself.

'Didn't you hear what I said? I want you out now.' He repeated himself slowly as though she was a backward child. 'And frankly I don't give a damn what James said or what James did, and I don't give a damn whether or not you sleep with my brother, as long as it isn't in my bed. Clear?'

'How dare you make such insinuations?' China spluttered, unable to hold her temper any longer. 'For your information, *Mr* Galloway, I have *not* slept with James, neither have I any intention of doing so, and ... and even if I had, I certainly would *not* choose your bed, you can rest assured. Those red sheets are revolting!' she finished, childish with fury.

His dark brows lifted fractionally at her outburst.

'Perhaps you were waiting for me then?' He took another step towards her, his face expressionless. 'As James is not here, perhaps I could provide an adequate substitute. After all, it's not every day I come home to find a naked woman in my shower.'

China knew then that he was laughing at her. 'That surprises me,' she muttered tartly. 'You certainly seem to think a lot of yourself. What makes you think you'd make an adequate substitute for James? I wouldn't touch you if you were the last man on earth—as far as I'm concerned you're totally and utterly resistable. Do I make myself clear?' she asked scathingly. Even as she said the words she knew deep inside herself that she was lying. He was a fiercely attractive man, and some treacherous part of her responded to his magnetic attraction even as she hated him, and this knowledge made her even angrier.

There was a certain open cynical amusement on his face as he listened to her.

'Playing hard to get?' he queried softly. Then as if a thought had struck him, he added, 'And if you didn't come here with James, how the hell did you get past the housekeeper, or is she another of James' fiascos?'

China took another deep breath. This was her chance. 'I am your housekeeper,' she said evenly. 'And if you'll only let me explain. . . .'

'Oh no,' Ben Galloway interrupted flatly, a faint spark of surprise in his eyes, 'spare me the sordid details. If this is my dear brother's idea of a joke, then I'm sorry, but you're sacked.'

He turned away, dismissing her, and China stared at his broad back, her face whitening, regretting everything she had said to him in anger. She knew that the situation looked damning, but if he would only let her explain.

Only an hour before, her life had been perfect and at last she had thought that her troubles were over. If she had to leave now, she had nowhere in the world to go. What would she do?

Ben Galloway turned round and looked at her.

'Didn't you hear what I said?' he asked patiently. 'You're sacked. I'll give you a reference and a month's pay, but you go—now.' His cold anger was gone, he was remote and businesslike.

'You can't sack me!' China whispered in horror.

'I just have,' he replied briskly.

Her chin lifted and she stared defiantly into his blank, golden eyes.

'I'm a very good housekeeper—look around the house. I'm a good cook too,' she added, remembering what James had said.

'Maybe you are,' his wide shoulders lifted uncaringly, 'but you're not suitable for me.'

'Why?' she questioned sadly.

'Do I have to spell it out to you? You're too young, too volatile and you're involved with my brother. Three good reasons to begin with,' he said coolly, the implication being that the list of her unsuitable qualities was too long to go into.

'Won't you even give me a chance?' she asked quietly. 'I can explain about the shower—it was all perfectly innocent.' He looked openly sceptical, but said nothing, so she continued,

'There's something wrong with the hot water system in my bathroom. I didn't think it would matter if I used your bathroom. I didn't expect you back——'

'That's more than obvious,' he cut in drily. 'But it makes no difference. Look, Miss. . . .'

'Harmon,' China quickly supplied.

'Miss Harmon. I'm tired, I'm hungry and I'm in no mood for long and involved explanations. If James gave you the wrong impression, then I'm sorry, but the fact remains that there's no job for you here.' He was talking slowly, implacably and to her over-sensitive ears he seemed to be enunciating every word with exaggerated patience.

She could not get round him. She would have to go.

She sighed, unable to stop the tears welling up in her eyes, and heard his angry exclamation.

'For God's sake, it's not the end of the world, you know. There are other jobs. What about your parents, you could surely live with them for a while until you get fixed up.'

China looked at him, her slow tears trickling down her pale face. 'I have no parents,' she whispered, wondering how he could be so cold, and so hard.

'Poor little orphan Annie,' he mocked unkindly, clearly not believing her.

China could not keep the pain out of her eyes any longer and she turned on her heel and rushed blindly for the door, tripping on the hem of her long night-dress. She would have fallen flat on her face if Ben Galloway had not moved quickly, surprisingly quickly for a man of his powerful physique, and caught her, his hands cruel and impatient as he set her on her feet again.

Without letting her go, he looked down at her for a long moment, taking in her white, tear-stained face and terribly hurt eyes.

He sighed heavily, swearing under his breath. 'Dear God, I'm sorry. I didn't mean to upset you, child.' He paused, then. 'Get dressed, fry some eggs, make some coffee and wait for me in the kitchen.' His voice was suddenly gentle and China's head jerked up, looking at him through the haze of her tears. Was he serious? It didn't matter, she would do as he told her and maybe they could sort something out from this awful mess.

She nodded, unable to speak, and ran downstairs, hurrying into her bedroom to change. She plaited her hair into a long pigtail down her back, to keep it out of the way, then dressed hurriedly in blue cotton trousers and blue woollen jumper, that unknown to her, brought out the startling colour of her eyes. Glancing at herself in the mirror, she was pleased with her reflection. She looked neat and efficient, but a little young. She did not think about Ben Galloway at all. She might hate him, but she needed this job, so it was better not to dwell on some of the unkind things he had said to her. Perhaps she could look round for another job, and perhaps—she crossed her fingers behind her back—he would let her stay on here until she found something.

I must keep a tight rein on my temper, she thought; whatever he says or does, I won't let him annoy me, I'll just be quiet and efficient, and with a bit of luck, I won't have to see much of him.

By the time she dashed into the kitchen, she was feeling a lot calmer. She shut Fortune out in the garden and began preparing breakfast.

When Ben Galloway appeared, she was sliding two perfectly-fried eggs on to a warm plate already containing bacon, sausage and mushrooms, and the aroma of freshly-brewed coffee was filling the kitchen.

She cast him a wary look as she placed the meal in front of him. He still looked exhausted, but fresher and more alert. He had shaved and his dark hair was damp from the shower. He had also changed into black trousers and a black, round-necked sweater.

He was dark and powerful and for some strange reason, China's heart turned over as he looked at her. She poured coffee for him and he actually managed a brief smile.

'This is good,' he said, indicating the food. 'Aren't you having anything to eat?' She shook her head. 'I couldn't . . . I'm not hungry,' she amended politely.

He got to his feet gracefully and fetched another cup from the dresser, then poured her some coffee and set it on the table opposite him.

'Sit down and drink,' he ordered.

China obeyed, and felt his dark unfathomable gaze on her as he finished his meal. She was pale and composed and she knew that he could read nothing in her face, which gave her confidence.

'Tell me about this job,' he said suddenly in that same expressionless voice she was becoming used to.

China set her cup back on the table so that he would not see the trembling of her fingers.

'I moved in yesterday,' she began in a small, carefully calm voice. 'James led me to believe that the job was mine. He telephoned you.' She stopped herself just in time. She did not want to sound accusing.

'How long have you known my brother?' he asked casually. China watched him as he poured out more coffee for them both. She did not want any more but did not dare to tell him so.

'Nearly two weeks,' she replied honestly.

'And how do you feel about him?' He stared at her as if trying to read her mind and she flushed brightly beneath that all-seeing gaze, a hot stain of colour rising over her face, condemning her.

'I see,' he said drily, misunderstanding her reaction.

He lit a cigarette, offering her one which she took. She needed something to do with her hands.

She did not answer him. He could think what he liked about her and James, he already thought the worst anyway. She glanced at him from beneath her lashes; he was leaning back in his chair, still watching her.

'We've met before,' she said, surprising herself with such an admission. He made her feel so nervous.

'Yes, I remember,' came the openly amused reply.

'I didn't think you did,' she said, trying to control the smile that was threatening to curve the corners of her mouth.

'You were wrong, then.' His voice had a strange softness to it.

China had expected a different answer, perhaps some sort of censure from him, but there was none. She stubbed out her cigarette and jumped to her feet.

'I'll clear away the dishes,' she said in bright, nervous tones.

'Sit down,' Ben Galloway ordered firmly. She subsided back into her seat and he said thoughtfully, 'James gave me to understand that you were an older woman. Can you explain that?'

China shrugged. 'He wanted to help me, I think.

I rather badly needed a job and somewhere to live. Please don't blame him,' she begged.

'Such loyalty,' he remarked, mocking her. 'And how did you find yourself in such an appalling situation?'

He obviously wanted to know her life story, although China resented the cold mockery in his voice.

'I know you didn't believe me before, but I am an orphan,' she told him, with a dignity that made it clear that she was not asking for sympathy.

'I'm sorry,' Ben Galloway said, sounding so sincere that she felt flustered.

'I had a job in Italy after school, but I had to leave.' She did not go into detail about the Cencellis. Ben Galloway already had a very low opinion of her morals, so he would probably blame her for what had happened. 'When I got back, I went to stay with my best friend, I met James through her, but she got married recently—and that's how I find myself in such an appalling situation,' she finished, repeating him word for word.

His mouth tightened, but he did not comment on her rudeness, he merely said, 'Can you speak Italian?'

China frowned at him in puzzlement. 'Of course.'

'Any other languages?'

'Only French, but why . . .?'

'I need a secretary, competent and fluent in at least two languages, to work from here. Do you type?'

'Yes, but. . . .'

'No buts, Miss Harmon.' He seemed to have come to a decision, his shrewd, intelligent mind working at full speed, and he was very businesslike and remote again. 'As it obviously means so much to you,

you can have the job, but I'll also require your services as a secretary. That will mean most mornings and any other time I need you. Understood? I don't keep office hours, but you will be well paid for any work you do for me.' He smiled for the first time since she had met him, and it took her breath away to see some warmth in his strong face. She was stunned by his words. She had expected him to kick her out, but now he was offering her two jobs and she fervently wished that she could turn him down flat and go away from Aspenmere Hall for ever. Every nerve, every instinct warned her of danger if she stayed.

Ben Galloway was a dangerous, attractive man, who she intensely disliked, and if she stayed, it seemed that she would be in close contact with him. It did not bear thinking about, but she had to accept his offer; there was nothing else.

Tears of self-pity filled her eyes, but she blinked them back furiously. She would survive and as soon as she could leave here she would, telling Ben Galloway exactly what she thought of him. It was something to look forward to, at least.

'Thank you, Mr Galloway, it's a deal,' she said, hating him and not daring to meet his eyes in case he saw her dislike and resentment.

He smiled, a clever, all-seeing smile as if he guessed how she was feeling.

'What's your first name?' he asked, quite gently.

'China,' she replied.

'A beautiful name, it suits you.' He sounded quite human for once.

'Thanks. It's my only link with my parents really,' she murmured, feeling quite flustered at his sudden kindness.

At that moment she heard Fortune scratching at the kitchen door.

'Oh dear! I forgot to tell you, Mr Galloway—I have a dog.' Her wide eyes beseeched Ben Galloway not to be angry with her. She got to her feet and opened the door, and the puppy bounded in immediately. 'Do you mind?'

He shook his head, holding his hand out to Fortune, who licked it enthusiastically.

'What the hell,' he said with laughter in his voice and in his golden eyes. 'This morning I was as free as a bird. Now I have an orphan housekeeper and her dog. Why should I mind?' He was teasing her, not unkindly, and for the first time China smiled at him, her eyes bright and innocently lovely. He stared at her, his eyes unfathomable, his attention fixed on her.

'I want you to call me Ben,' he said suddenly, and China's eyes widened.

'Okay,' she agreed readily, watching him as he got to his feet.

'I have to get some sleep, I'll see you later,' he said gently, and then he was gone.

China sat at the table for long moments, feeling confused and rather happy. Whatever else this job was going to be, it would surely be interesting.

CHAPTER FOUR

BEN GALLOWAY slept late into the afternoon, and the telephone rang for him a number of times. China had just finished washing the dishes when it rang for the first time.

It was a woman with a low, husky voice, obviously surprised at China picking up the phone. The woman on the other end made it clear that she *had* to speak to Ben Galloway, so China decided to see if he was awake. Asking the woman to hold the line, she ran quickly upstairs and knocked on his bedroom door. There was no answer, so tentatively she pushed open the door and peeped inside. The red blinds were closed and the room was very dim, but in the semi-darkness she could see that Ben was asleep. He lay sprawled on the bed, his wide brown shoulders bare and somehow sensual against the satin sheets.

He was breathing deeply and evenly, and without conscious thought. China found herself silently moving nearer to him, into the room, until she stood at the side of the bed, looking down at him, hardly daring to breathe for fear of waking him, her eyes riveted on his face.

He looked younger, kinder, his face less harsh in sleep. His long dark hair fell back against the pillow and to her own surprise China found herself committing every inch of his strong face to memory.

Her eyes lingered on the hollows beneath his eyelids and beneath his prominent cheekbones, on his firm, relaxed mouth and strong, well-defined chin, and with horror found her heart beating faster as

61

she looked at him. It was ridiculous, she did not even like him.

Then she remembered the husky-voiced woman on the telephone and had to control the giggle that was bubbling into her throat. She knew one thing for certain, and that was the fact that she did not dare to wake Ben, so tiptoeing out of the room and pulling the door closed as quietly as she could, she ran downstairs and told the caller that she would have to leave a message because Mr Galloway could not be disturbed. The woman on the other end was not pleased, but there was nothing she could do, so she gave her message and slammed down the receiver.

China whistled softly under her breath, wondering what—she looked down at the notepad on the table—Olivia looked like. I expect she's beautiful, she thought wryly, catching a glance of herself in the mirror above the telephone and sighing discontentedly. Ben Galloway's lovers would all be very possessive of him, she did not doubt. Pulling herself together with a visible effort before she started sliding into a fantasy about him, she strolled back into the kitchen to make up a shopping list.

It was after four by the time she got back from the shops. She parked the Mini at the back of the house again and staggered indoors with two laden baskets, feeling hot and tired, only to find Ben making coffee and idly flicking through a newspaper in the kitchen.

He looked up as she entered the room, walking over to her and taking the baskets from her unresisting fingers.

'I can manage,' she protested, wondering at the weakness in her stomach as she looked at him, and unsuccessfully trying to put it down to lack of food.

He looked much better for his sleep, strong and relaxed, the bruised shadows beneath his eyes almost gone. She wondered how old he was. She guessed about thirty-five, thirty-six, although it was difficult to tell. He ignored her protest and put down the baskets on the table.

'You look as though you're about to drop,' he remarked honestly, staring at her through narrowed eyes.

He poured out two cups of coffee and China sank gratefully into a chair, wondering why she was being so awkward with him. She knew as well as he did that she could not have managed the baskets for very much longer. Her reaction to him was always so defensive.

They sat in silence, drinking the coffee he had made. China felt very tired. It had been a long day, she thought, stifling a yawn.

Ben raised an eyebrow, missing nothing. 'Do you think this job will be too much for you?' he asked quietly, his blank eyes resting on her slender wrists as she tried to rub some life back into them. China sighed. 'I know we didn't get off to a very good start . . .' she began, misunderstanding him and feeling irritated at his constant needling.

He silenced her, holding up his hands, a slight smile playing at the corners of his mouth.

'Okay, you irritable child, don't fly into a temper! Forget I spoke.'

Not easy, China thought to herself, lowering her eyes and concentrating on her coffee.

'Did you get your telephone messages?' she asked a few seconds later, wanting to break the strangely tense silence that was winding around them and filling the kitchen.

Ben nodded, still amused. 'Very efficient,' he

mocked her gently. She flashed him a dark look and got to her feet, starting to unpack her provisions. Why couldn't he just be polite? It was not going to be easy to stick to a purely employer-employee relationship if she kept losing her temper with him, which she surely would if he kept on at her this way.

She stored away some fresh fish in the refrigerator. 'Will you be here for dinner?' she asked politely, thinking of the telephone call from Olivia and hoping that he would be out.

He looked up from his newspaper. 'Yes. Disappointed?' he asked shrewdly, his amber eyes piercing on her face, watching her easily-read expression.

'I have to know because of the food,' she answered stiffly, trying to be polite. She felt confused by the conflicting emotions inside her. She wanted him to go out, to leave her alone, but she was inexplicably glad that he would not be spending the evening with the undoubtedly lovely Olivia.

'Of course you do,' he said blandly, managing to give the impression that he knew exactly what she was thinking. He got to his feet, flexing his powerful shoulder muscles, drawing China's unwilling eyes to the strength of his body.

He reached over and ran a lean, careless finger down her cheek.

'It's good to know that you're so conscientious,' he said softly, and turning on his heel, left the room.

China watched him go with wide eyes, her hand to her cheek where he had touched her. Her skin burned as though his fingers had been fire. Damn him! she thought fiercely.

Some hours later, she set the table in the dining room, laughing at her distorted reflection in the polished wood of the table. She had lit fires in all the rooms because the evening was very chilly, and it gave her a hitherto unknown sense of belonging to switch on the lamps and pull closed the curtains.

She had not seen Ben since he left the kitchen, but she knew that he had been working in his study all afternoon. She smiled now as she admired the heavy silver cutlery around the solitary place setting. Everything was under control in the kitchen and she knew that the meal would be delicious. It was about time he learned that she could do something properly.

She turned to leave the room and saw him standing in the doorway, blocking her exit, watching her as she worked and sang to herself. His amber eyes flicked over the shining, carefully-laid table, and back to her again.

'Eat with me, China. I don't care to eat alone,' he said in that low, persuasive voice that shivered along her nerve endings, using her christian name for the first time. It sounded good on his lips.

'I can eat in the kitchen,' she stammered, surprised by his request.

He smiled. 'Afraid?' he taunted softly, and she flushed, feeling the familiar flare of irritation inside herself.

'Of course not,' she said tautly, not daring to look into his face.

'Set another place, then,' he ordered bleakly. 'After all, you can always pretend that you're dining with James.'

She felt hurt by that cruel remark, and her soft mouth tightened as she pulled some more cutlery out of the drawer and barely restraining herself from slamming it down, set another place, as far away from his as possible.

He watched the unconscious grace of her body as

she moved around the table, her hair glinting dull gold as the light caught it and her pure wide eyes bright with anger. Having finished at the table, she turned to leave the room, but he still did not move from the doorway.

'Excuse me,' she said as acidly as she could, which was difficult because she found that her eyes were welling up with ridiculous, frustrated tears.

Ben did not move a muscle but stood perfectly still, staring down at her lowered head with hooded eyes.

China was so near to tears that she could not speak, her heart stopping altogether for one suffocating second as he caught her chin in long, hard-skinned fingers and tilted her face up towards his own.

He saw the tears shining in her eyes and his mouth tightened. 'What is it? Does the thought of having dinner with me strike such fear into your heart?' he teased gently, trying to coax her into a better humour.

She stared into his eyes, catching her breath at the tenderness she saw shining in the clear, amber depths.

'Why are you always so unkind?' she whispered miserably, trying to swallow back her tears.

'Have I been unkind to you?' he asked wonderingly, his mouth twisting as he stared into her hurt face. 'Would you want my kindness, China?'

She shivered at something in his low voice.

'I don't know,' she answered honestly, and he smiled, lifting his other hand to gently flick away her tears.

'I don't think you would,' he murmured, and lowered his dark head very slowly to brush her mouth with cool, gentle lips.

As their mouths touched, China shuddered, an arrow of pleasure mingled with pain, shooting through her body. She wanted his strong arms around her, wanted his kiss to deepen, wanted him to want her. ... It was a shocking admission, and she pulled herself away from him with a stifled cry and fled from the room.

As she showered and changed for dinner, the touch of Ben's mouth was still imprinted on her senses. She touched her mouth with faintly trembling fingers as she considered her appearance in the mirror. The violet cashmere dress looked sophisticated and expensive and it clung to her shapely, slender figure, its colour darkening the pure blue of her eyes.

She left her hair loose and applied mascara and lip gloss. She looked good, even if she was a little afraid to face Ben Galloway. She practised facial expressions as she stepped into her high-heeled shoes, trying for a look of remote calmness. She could not manage it, he was too astute to be fooled, anyway. Her emotions seemed to be very shaky today, more than once she had nearly burst into tears.

She strolled into the kitchen trying to quell the nerves that were fluttering in her stomach at the thought of spending so much time with Ben this evening, and began to drain the vegetables. She sensed rather than saw him appear beside her. That was another of his irritating habits, the way he moved so silently, so gracefully and quickly that she never could be sure when she was alone.

'Let me help,' he urged, smiling at her. He had changed too, into a superbly-cut maroon velvet dinner jacket and dark trousers, his white ruffled shirt startling against his tanned skin. He looked big and dark and dangerous, and she felt her mouth go dry as she cast him a brief, startled look.

'There's not much to do now—besides, I'm getting paid to do it,' she said lightly but firmly.

'As you wish. I'll see to the wine,' he replied, sounding faintly irritated. 'You look very beautiful,' he added with a slow smile.

'Thank you.' China turned back to the sink, blushing furiously at his compliment, and determined not to let him see how easily he could affect her.

The meal, thank goodness, was perfect and to her own surprise China found herself relaxing, smiling at Ben's deliberately amusing conversation. He was very charming, effortlessly putting her at ease. The wine helped too, it tasted innocuous enough, but when she got up to fetch the dessert, a mouthwatering lemon mousse that she had made earlier, she felt her head spinning slightly.

As Ben talked, she stared into his lean, hard-boned face with wonder and an attraction she was finding increasingly difficult to fight. I don't even like him, she kept telling herself in a desperate attempt to force her shining eyes, to say nothing of her attention, away from him.

Ben made coffee when the meal was over, insisting that she had done enough, so she sat back in luxury by the roaring fire, gazing into the bright flames feeling relaxed and more content than she could remember feeling for a very long time.

She smiled at Ben with her happiness openly in her face as he brought the tray of coffee to her side, and she saw him stiffen, almost imperceptibly, his eyes sharpening on her, dark and enigmatic.

'That was a fantastic meal,' he remarked lazily, when the coffee was poured and they both held cigarettes.

'I told you I could cook,' China replied with an impish smile.

Ben laughed. 'So you did. I guess I wasn't really listening. You're a strange girl, China—tell me why somebody like you is willing to be shut away, housekeeping in an old barn of a house like this,' he added curiously.

'I like housekeeping, and I think it's a beautiful old house, but the main attraction for me is the flat. I've never had rooms of my own before. . . .' She broke off suddenly. He would not understand.

'I think I would,' he said softly, and she realised that she had been speaking aloud.

Her face coloured with embarrassment and she did not know what to say.

'You blush very easily,' he murmured, not taking his eyes off her sweet face.

'I'm sorry,' China said lamely. 'It's not a criticism, merely an observation.' He was exasperated and amused.

She glanced up at him as he drew deeply on his cigarette, his dark eyes narrowed against the smoke that veiled his strong face. He was affecting her very deeply, his sexual magnetism drawing her to him, almost against her will. She had never been so attracted to a man before and it was very disturbing, all the more disturbing because she could feel her initial dislike of him dissolving, and if she did not dislike him, she would have no defence against him.

She drank her coffee quickly and got to her feet, intending to wash the dishes and then retire to bed, making a sudden decision to keep out of Ben Galloway's way as much as possible. Easier said than done!

'Leave the dishes, I'll see to them,' Ben said firmly as she began piling them on to a tray.

China glanced at him. 'There's no need, they won't take me long,' she replied, just as firmly, continuing with her task.

'You've worked hard today and I appreciate it, so leave them,' he said in that patient voice that always rubbed her up the wrong way.

'I want to do them,' she argued childishly, glaring at him.

'You're so damned contrary,' Ben snapped coldly. 'Even I can see that you're exhausted. For God's sake do as you're told for once!'

China flinched from the harsh words.

'That's just the point,' she began angrily. 'I want my position here to be crystal clear. You pay me for housekeeping duties, and washing dishes is one of those duties. I'm not your servant, I'm a paid employee—paid to wash the dishes. Okay?' She did not dare to look at him because she knew that he was very angry now.

He got to his feet, his lean face hard and cold. 'You make yourself very clear,' he said icily, and left the room. China continued loading the tray with shaking hands, feeling unutterably miserable. It had been such a pleasant evening; why had she spoiled it?

She washed the dishes carefully, concentrating all her attention on them, and when all the work was done she switched out the kitchen lights and made her way to her bedroom. She would go to bed. Ben was right, as always; she was exhausted and it had been one hell of a day. Perhaps tomorrow would be better, she thought, childishly crossing her fingers underneath the bedclothes.

It took her a long time to get to sleep. She lay in the large bed, twisting restlessly against the smooth sheets. However hard she strained her ears she could not hear any movement in the rest of the house, and assumed that Ben was working in his study.

When she did finally doze off, she was troubled by nightmares, vague dark dreams that made her cry out with fear, and pleated her sleeping forehead with frowning anguish.

She was dreaming of Italy, of Signor Cencilli reaching for her with dark, ugly lust in his eyes. She could not get away from him and she was screaming, screaming. . . .

She woke with a start to find herself fighting with Ben, whose hands were on her shoulders as he tried to calm her. She looked up into his face as he leaned over her, and reality slowly crept back into her fearful mind. His eyes were narrowed and concerned, the stark lines of his face dramatic in the dim light from the window.

'Ben——' she whispered his name to herself, drawing in deep, shaky breaths to try and stop her heart pounding so heavily.

'It was only a dream, you're safe now,' he told her, his voice curiously gentle. He reached out and snapped on the bedside lamp. China let her head fall back against the soft pillows, weary with relief, and looked at him.

He was wearing a black silk robe, open at the neck to reveal his hard, hair-roughened chest and short enough to expose strong, muscular legs. She sighed, pushing her hair away from her face.

'I'm sorry,' she said shakily, her mouth suddenly dry at his nearness.

He smiled at her in reassurance. 'There's nothing to be sorry about. What were you dreaming about?' he asked quietly.

She hesitated for a moment, wondering whether or not to tell him.

'Something that happened in Italy,' she finally whispered, turning her face away from him.

He caught her chin and turned her head towards him again.

'Tell me,' he prompted.

Looking into his dark gentle eyes, China knew that she trusted him, that she wanted to tell him.

'I worked as a nanny in Rome—I enjoyed it. Adele, the woman I worked for, was a good friend and the children were beautiful.' Her eyes were far-away as she reminisced. 'But Signor Cencelli made ... made a pass at me ... it was so horrible. He turned very nasty when I wouldn't. .... Adele found him trying to ... trying to.....' China found that she could not say the words that described what had happened and her eyes were filling with sad tears. 'She sacked me, she was one of the best friends I ever had.....'

Ben sighed heavily, his eyes dark with anger, his mouth tight.

'And you still dream about it?' It was more of a statement than a question.

China nodded. 'In my dreams I can't get away from him.' Her tears were pouring down her face and she wondered for a second why she was telling him all this.

He touched his hand to her face. 'My poor love,' he said very softly, wiping away her tears with incredibly gentle fingers. It was the last straw, something inside her snapped and she found his tender concern almost unbearable, the strained floodgates of her tears bursting, as she began to sob.

She longed for Ben's comfort, and as if he could read her mind, he groaned suddenly and pulled her into the strong warm circle of his arms, stroking back her hair and murmuring soothing words that strangely comforted her as she pressed her hot face against the smooth, cool skin of his shoulder.

He held her until her tears dried, then he wiped her face and lowered her back against the high mound of pillows. He got to his feet in one lithe, easy movement.

'I'll make you something to drink,' he said with a smile. 'It will help you to sleep.'

'Ben——' She was afraid of being left alone, and it showed.

'I'll only be a couple of minutes, you can shout to me while I'm boiling the milk,' he teased reassuringly, touching her small, pale face, his eyes concerned.

Then he was gone, and China felt so alone that she *did* want to call him back. Her only consolation was that she could hear him whistling as he moved about the kitchen. He was doing it so that she would not be afraid, and a warm glow settled around her heart at his kindness.

Moments later, as promised, he reappeared, holding out a mug of steaming chocolate to her.

'Drink,' he said firmly. 'Every last drop of it.'

He sat down on the edge of the bed and watched her with unfathomable eyes as she held the cup to her mouth. The chocolate was delicious, warm and sweet and somehow comforting.

'You're very kind,' she said in a small voice, her blue eyes enormous in her tear-stained face as she looked at him.

'You didn't think so earlier this evening,' Ben said drily. She opened her mouth to protest, but before she could speak he said, 'Drink your chocolate, don't talk. It will do you no good at all if it's cold.'

She did as she was told, then handed him back the mug, licking her lips, unaware that she was drawing attention to her vulnerable mouth, unaware that his hooded eyes rested on her lips.

She felt very drowsy, but there was still a ball of cold fear in her stomach at the thought of going back to sleep. Ben leaned over and touched his mouth to her forehead.

'Sleep now, child,' he said, getting to his feet.

'Did I wake you?' China asked quickly, not wanting to let him go.

'You called for me,' he replied, and China flushed. Had she called his name? It was rather embarrassing, hardly the sort of thing that was expected from a housekeeper.

'I wasn't asleep,' Ben added laughingly, noting the hot colour in her cheeks.

'I'm sorry,' China whispered, feeling very foolish. 'I didn't mean to disturb you.'

'I know.' He stood by the door now, about to leave, and before she thought about the possible consequences of such a request, governed only by her fear of being left alone in the dark, China said quickly,

'Ben, please don't leave me, stay with me.' Her beautiful eyes pleaded with him and for a moment he froze, shock-still.

'China, you don't know what you're asking,' he said in a low voice, raking his hand through his thick dark hair.

'I shouldn't have asked—it was stupid of me. I'm sorry,' she whispered, cursing the tears of utter loneliness that were threatening to overwhelm her again.

'For God's sake, stop apologising!' Ben snapped angrily, and the next moment he was beside her again, swearing softly under his breath as he took her into his arms. China lay trembling against him, gradually relaxing against the hard warmth of his body, the strong steady beat of his heart beneath her cheek. She didn't want to go to sleep, she wanted to savour his nearness, his strength, but she was so very tired. . . .

She woke at dawn to find herself still lying against Ben's chest, the heavy muscles of his arms still coiled protectively around her. She did not move for a second as the events of the night before flooded back into her drowsy memory. Ben was still sleeping, his chest moving deeply and steadily up and down beneath her cheek. His skin was warm.

The room was filled with pale weak light and without moving her head, she could see her painting on the opposite wall. Her eyes fixed on the bright colours as she wondered what to do. A small sigh of contentment escaped her; it was so good to be in his arms. This thought crept unbidden into her mind and she stopped herself short. What a crazy thing to think! He was cold and arrogant and she did not like him, and yet she was lying here in his arms after spending the night in the same bed. It was madness. She felt a bubble of hysteria rising up in her throat and had to fight to control herself from laughing out loud and waking him.

Too late. Some small movement had alerted him and he woke slowly, his arms tightening round her in an instinctively protective gesture.

China moved her head and looked up into his face. He was staring down at her with warm, lazy eyes, and her breath caught in her throat at something she saw in his face. She wanted to say something witty and cool that would make him laugh and would put this ridiculous situation into perspective, but she couldn't think of a thing, and her tongue seemed stuck to the roof of her mouth.

'Good morning, China,' he said lazily, his voice a

husky caress, still not letting her go.

China was silent. Did he say that to all his lovers when they woke up in his arms the morning after? She doubted it. They would wake languorous and satisfied, not frustrated like her. She did not doubt that he was an expert lover. She bit her lip fiercely, tasting blood, at such shocking thoughts. What on earth was the matter with her?

'Lost your tongue?' Ben queried softly.

'If you must know, I'm embarrassed,' she replied in a muffled voice.

He laughed at that.

'I don't think it's very funny,' she said painfully, not having the courage to meet his eyes. She tried to free herself, needing to get away from him, but his arms were bands of steel and he would not release her.

'You look beautiful in the morning light,' he remarked in an expressionless voice.

'I don't think that's funny either,' she snapped, lying still now, knowing the futility of trying to fight his superior strength.

'It wasn't supposed to be. Are you always so bad-tempered in the morning?' he asked softly, his mouth moving against her pale hair.

'Why are you making fun of me, and why won't you let me go?' China demanded, trying to ignore the sudden pounding of her heart.

'I'm not making fun of you, and I enjoy holding you in my arms,' he laughed in answer.

She was infuriated, frightened of her response to him. If this was his idea of a joke. . . .

'I hate you!' she said vehemently. 'Let me go. Now!'

His mouth thinned ominously, and she knew by the stiffening of his powerful body that she had gone too far.

'You seem to forget, sweetheart, that you invited me to stay,' he said coolly.

China's head jerked up and she stared into his hard face with wide, frightened eyes.

'No,' she whispered, as his hand came up to tangle in the thickness of her hair, holding her still as he lowered his head and found her mouth with his own.

His kiss was warm and angry, parting her lips with fierce expertise, as he held her struggling body effortlessly against the hard wall of his chest. Her hands were trapped between them, splayed against the hair-roughened skin, and she could feel his heartbeat racing away beneath her fingers.

His kiss was shattering and although she fought against it, she could feel herself shamelessly responding to the urgency of his mouth as it moved against hers.

A second later she was free, as Ben released her from his arms and lay back against the pillows, cupping his hands behind his head, a kind of enforced stillness stiffening his body.

'Damn you, China. You make me so angry,' he muttered wearily.

She touched her fingers to her bruised lips. 'I don't mean to,' she whispered shakily, achingly aware of his strong, muscular body only inches away from her own.

As he had kissed her, the strangest, unknown things had happened deep inside her, piercing sensations had filled her body, weakening her resistance to him, and her blood had flowed faster, heating in her veins, as he had purged his anger against the soft innocence of her mouth. She had not wanted him to draw back, she had wanted him to make love to her.

She shook her head, and realised that he was looking at her. She coloured, embarrassed by her own thoughts.

'Can you read my mind?' she asked wonderingly, half able to believe that he could.

'I wish I could,' he replied, with amusement in his voice. China sighed, relieved at his answer.

'That's good,' she said, half to herself.

'If you could read my mind, you'd know that I want you,' Ben said, so casually that the implications of his remark didn't sink in for a moment.

When they did, China's head jerked upwards and she stared at him, dry mouthed, her heart pounding.

'I . . . you'd better go,' she whispered in a shaking voice.

Ben smiled, a thin, humourless twisting of his lips.

'Yes, I better had,' he replied harshly. He got off the bed and strolled towards the door. Then he was gone, and China huddled beneath the bedclothes, trembling with shock and the weakness that was flooding her body.

Ben Galloway wanted her. It was the craziest, most amazing thing she had ever heard, and trying to control the erratic pounding of her heart, she told herself and the empty room, 'I hate him.'

Vehemently spoken, it sounded hollow and untruthful even to her own ears.

CHAPTER FIVE

'WE have two guests coming to stay today,' Ben announced a couple of mornings later as China served breakfast. 'I don't know how long they'll stay. Can you cope?' He gave her a brief hard smile.

'Yes, of course I can,' China replied calmly, returning his smile with vagueness as she wondered who these two guests would be. 'How many rooms shall I prepare, and will they be here for dinner?'

'Such an orderly mind,' Ben mocked gently. 'One double room, I think, and yes, they will be here for dinner.'

'Right.' She made herself sound businesslike and turned to leave the room, but his hand on her arm detained her.

'You're looking very tired, child,' he commented softly, taking in the bruised shadows beneath her eyes and her pale skin, with concern.

'I'm fine,' China lied easily, because she had no intention of telling him how difficult she had been finding it to sleep at nights. Her attitudes and feelings for him had changed over the past few days and she found that she could not dislike him any more. Images of him crowded her mind practically all the time and she would lie restlessly in the darkness of her bedroom haunted by the memory of that night spent in his arms. He had offered her comfort of the worst kind, a comfort that had drawn her to him, trapping her with her longing for him.

The more she was getting to know him, the more he intrigued her. He was wealthy and very successful, and he also had an intelligent retentive mind that worked at a speed that China sometimes found frightening. He was strong and rather ruthless, self-assured and charming. But there was a gentle, caring side to his personality and this, coupled with a devastating sexual magnetism made him far too disturbing, both physically and intellectually, for her peace of mind.

'Fine, but too damned stubborn for your own good,' Ben remarked, still staring at her with those shrewd amber eyes.

China felt almost naked under his slow thorough scrutiny and twisted away from him in panic, afraid of what he might see in her eyes.

'Why don't you leave me alone?' she muttered defensively, weakened by his concern.

She left the kitchen, finding herself trembling all over as she stood in the hall with one nervous hand pressed to her tightening stomach. Walking to the front door, she pulled it open and looked outside. It was a cold, crisp morning, the ground thick with silvery frost, the sky bright with weak sunlight.

She had to get out of the house for a while. She would go for a walk, clear her head and try to get Ben out of her system for a few hours.

She collected her fur jacket, tugging bright woollen gloves out of her pocket, and slipped on her boots, then called to Fortune, who ran to her immediately, jumping up and down and whining loudly as he saw the lead in her hand.

China stepped out into the morning air, gulping in deep clean breaths of cold air. It was good to be outside, there was an illusion of freedom and she had felt almost claustrophobic in the house this morning. Ben had nothing to do with that, of course, it was her. He was behaving perfectly, cool and polite, friendly, yet keeping a distance between them. Perfectly.

The sound of a car pulling down the drive alerted her. She hoped it was Ben's guests, he would have to see to them himself. But she was wrong; it was James.

China smiled at him, surprised at how happy she was to see him. He was so uncomplicated and light-hearted, just the tonic she needed. He jumped out of the car and took both her hands, leaning over to kiss her cheek.

'Hello, love. How are you, and how's the job?'

'I'm fine, and the job. . . .' China pulled an expressive face.

James laughed. 'Ben's slave-driving you already, huh?'

'Well——' China began, half-jokingly.

'Tell him, China. I'll be interested to hear how you think I'm treating you,' cut in a cool, slightly sardonic voice from behind them.

China flushed brightly, profoundly glad that he could not see her face. James saw the hot stain of colour on her cheeks, though, and his mild eyes narrowed speculatively.

'Ben! Great to see you, brother!' He left China's side to shake Ben's hand. 'How long have you been back?'

'A couple of days.' Ben's voice was low and amused, and China could feel his eyes upon her and did not dare to turn round to face him.

'I'm going for a walk,' she said quietly, aiming her voice somewhere between the two men.

She whistled to Fortune and began to walk away. Seconds later, James caught up with her.

'Hey, wait for me!' he laughed.

'I thought you'd come to see Ben,' China commented, without malice, stopping to wait for him.

'Silly girl, I came to see you,' James told her with a smile, playfully flicking at her hair.

'Oh.' China digested this slowly, her eyes on the ghostly, frosted trees. Then she said, 'How's your job, still working yourself to death?'

James smiled excitedly. 'Good news, actually. That's what I've come to tell you. A friend of mine, the guy that gave me a lift at Clare and Paul's wedding, remember?' China nodded, '—well, he and I are going into partnership. We've bought a hotel in Athens and we're going to run it together.' His young face was flushed with enthusiasm.

'It's a big change from your usual work, isn't it?' China asked, dazed by his news.

He shrugged. 'I guess so. I'll be attending to the financial side of things at the hotel, of course, but I need a change. I'm beginning to feel stifled here,' he admitted ruefully.

'Perhaps you're more like your father than you imagine,' China said gently.

'Maybe. All I know is that it's a great opportunity, a new life.'

She reached down and picked up a dry twig to throw for Fortune, who bounded clumsily after it, making her smile.

James had a restless streak in him that she had never noticed before, and could not understand. She had imagined him to be settled here, he was building up his business, he had a home—it seemed a little crazy to her to give up such security. It must be my orphanage upbringing, she thought wryly.

'When will you go?' she asked, feeling sad to be losing such a good friend, but at the same time glad for him, because it was what he wanted to do.

'As soon as possible,' James replied, revealing his

impatience. 'I don't really know for sure. I flew back from Athens this morning—that's why I haven't been to see you these past couple of days. But as soon as I can tie things up here, I'll be off!'

'I'll miss you,' China told him sadly. 'You've been such a good friend.'

'Will you?' James looked pleased, hastily adjusting his expression as she punched him lightly on the arm.

'You know what I mean.'

'I'll miss you too . . . in fact, why don't you come with me? There'll be plenty of work for a talented girl like you.'

China laughed, flattered by his offer.

'I'm serious, love. If you want a job, come with me.' He put his arm through hers, persuasively, but she shook her head.

'I have a job,' she said lightly, suddenly frightened to find that the thought of leaving Ben pained her.

'Well, the offer's always there. By the way, how are you getting on with Ben?'

'Not very well,' China admitted, lowering her eyes.

'Why?' he asked bluntly, watching her carefully.

She shrugged delicately. 'Oh, I don't know. I seem to make him angry all the time, and he's so cold. . . .' To her horror, she could not finish her sentence because the next second she burst into tears, surprising herself, but surprising James more.

He slipped his arm round her shoulder and squeezed her, obviously at a loss to know what to do.

China wiped away her tears with trembling, furious fingers. 'Oh dear, I'm sorry,' she moaned, angry with herself for being so silly, and angry because she had obviously embarrassed James. She could only assume that she was feeling so emotional because she was not sleeping properly. 'I'm just tired and overwrought, and I didn't mean to embarrass you,' she muttered, finally managing to control her damnable tears.

'You haven't embarrassed me,' James said gallantly, but she could see that he was lying. There was a faint wariness in his eyes, an uncomfortable colour in his face, and for the first time she wondered why he had never attempted to kiss her properly. A ridiculous thought, because she had never wanted anything from James except friendship, so why should she feel so piqued about getting what she wanted? I suppose he just doesn't find me attractive, she thought unreasonably, her heart thumping painfully fast as she remembered Ben's kiss and the warm sensual anger in his lips.

James was talking and she forced herself out of her reverie to pay attention. 'I'm sorry?' she apologised, staring at him with questioning eyes.

'We'd better get back. Fortune has worn himself out and big brother will be wondering where you are. He won't take kindly to you being out with me when you should have your nose to the grindstone.'

'I'm sure he won't mind,' China protested, crossing her fingers. In point of fact, she wouldn't put anything past Ben Galloway.'

They strolled back to the house, arm in arm, chatting together, followed by a weary Fortune who was having trouble keeping up with them. China filled her lungs with the clear morning air, feeling happy, stopping to pick up some leaf skeletons she found on the ground.

James had someone coming to view his flat and so declined China's offer of coffee. She waved to him as the car shot down the drive, spraying gravel in its wake, then went inside.

As James had predicted, Ben was angry. He met her in the hall as she was struggling out of her fur jacket. She smiled at him, unselfconsciously, her small face flushed with becoming colour from the sharp wind, and held out her gloved hand.

'Look, leaf skeletons. Aren't they lovely?'

The amber eyes flashed anger at her, his mouth a thin, hard line.

'Perhaps, but I don't pay you to collect bloody leaf skeletons,' he snapped coldly. China stared at him, mesmerised by the hard-boned beauty of his face.

'I ... I only went for a short walk,' she stammered, surprised by his fury.

'There's a pile of Italian notes in the study, waiting to be typed. I don't have the time to waste while you leave the house for "short walks" with my brother,' Ben snapped, his narrowed eyes frozen on her face.

His words angered her. 'I think you're being rather unreasonable, *Mr* Galloway. I'm not psychic, I had no idea about those notes,' she said heatedly. 'And if I remember correctly, it was *you* who said that you don't work office hours.'

'When there's work to be done, I expect you to get on with it,' Ben told her darkly, raking an impatient hand through the thickness of his hair, his movements stretching the silken material of his shirt, tautly across his broad, muscular shoulders.

'Very well, I'll start now,' China said furiously. 'And I'll work until they're all finished. Will that suit you, or do you want a grovelling apology as well, *sir*?' She was faintly shocked at her own insolence, but he made her so *angry*. He had destroyed her pleasant mood so carelessly with a few harsh, unreasonable words. He was utterly heartless!

She had gone too far though, this time, and she gasped as Ben's fingers closed on her shoulders in a cruel, tight grip. He shook her slightly, making her wince.

'You little bitch!' he grated, the harsh lines of his mouth twisted with anger and ice. He pulled her hard against him and cupped her pointed chin, slowly lowering his head until their mouths touched and he kissed her fiercely, purging himself of his anger until she could taste blood in her mouth.

Shocked by his brutality, China swayed against his hard body, wondering fleetingly if she had subconsciously and deliberately goaded him into doing this.

A second later his kiss changed, becoming seeking, demanding, as with a muffled groan he closed his arms around her, his hands becoming gentle as he reached to caress her slim white throat.

She melted submissively against him, a warm, sensual weakness flooding her body, relaxing her against his taut strength. Of their own volition, her hands moved up to his shoulders, moving over the powerful muscles in tentative caress and up again to tangle in the darkness of his hair, drawing him closer to her, wanting never to let him go.

'China,' he murmured her name, as his warm, hungry mouth moved across her face in slow, caressing exploration. 'Dear God, you drive me crazy, do you know that?' He groaned, his arms tightening around her, holding her so tightly that her feet were not touching the ground.

China laughed breathlessly, glad that his anger was gone.

A discreet cough behind them heralded the arrival of Mrs Stephenson, who clucked her tongue disapprovingly as she saw them wrapped in each other's arms. China did not mistake the twinkle in the older woman's eye, though, as she moved past them, unbuttoning her coat.

' 'Morning, Mr Galloway, China.'

'Mrs Stephenson.' Ben inclined his head, his mouth gentle.

'Hello,' China added, unable to keep her amusement out of her voice.

Ben released her then, kissing both her cheeks with lingering tenderness.

'The typing,' China remembered, flashing him a bright smile.

'Coffee first, I think,' Ben said firmly, taking her hand and leading her into the kitchen, where Mrs Stephenson was already plugging in the percolater. China glanced at Ben, to find he was looking at her and their eyes locked, holding them both in a world that contained only them. China's eyes were wide, pure and free of deceit as she stared into the flaming golden depths of his, seeing his hunger for her and a certain gentleness that made her catch her breath.

It was a timeless, frozen moment that seemed to last for ever, until Mrs Stephenson broke between them, shouting loud profanities at Fortune, whose muddy paws had made an unholy mess on the kitchen floor.

They all sat together to drink their coffee. China liked Mrs Stephenson, who although inclined to be dour, had a heart of gold. There was something solid and nonsense-free about her and she could enthrall China for hours on end with tales of her family.

China longed to ask her about Ben, she found that her curiosity and interest in him knew no bounds, but she felt that it might not be quite right. She was hoping that one day soon Mrs Stephenson might expand on that subject with no prompting from her. The odds were certainly for it, because Mrs Stephenson seemed very fond of gossip, and China knew more about certain people in the village than she imagined they did themselves.

She watched Ben from beneath her lashes as she held her coffee cup between her hands, warming her icy fingers. He was chatting to Mrs Stephenson, asking about her family and telling her that he might have some work for her eldest son, Geoff, who was the bane of that lady's life. She continued watching, awed by his masculine beauty, her eyes riveted on the stark lines of his face.

He was smiling now, his eyes warm and frankly charming, and as though sensing her scrutiny of him, he lifted his dark brows at her, some unrecognisable emotion darkening his eyes for a second, before he smiled at her. China smiled back, feeling a warmth around her heart.

All too soon it was time to start work, and she followed Ben into the study. The fire was lit, scenting the room with the fragrance of burning wood, its lights dancing off the mellow oak panelling.

Ben had fixed up a desk with a typewriter on it, opposite to his. This arrangement did not particularly suit China, as it was far too distracting and sometimes quite embarrassing to be working in such close proximity. Every time she lifted her head she would see him—far too disturbing.

'Now, these notes. . . .' he began, only to be interrupted by the telephone. China watched him as he talked on the phone, watched his smooth, animal grace as he walked around the desk to collect some papers from a drawer. He was wearing tight jeans in denim that fitted his lean hips and muscular thighs like a second skin, and a dark silk shirt, open at his brown throat, that emphasised his tanned, good looks and strangely-coloured eyes.

He had a superb physique, tall and powerful— the sort of body, so China had read in women's magazines, that sent women weak at the knees. And I'm no exception, she thought ruefully, pulling herself together and feeding a number of sheets of typing paper and carbon into the machine in front of her.

She found the translation from English into Italian very easy and quite enjoyable and was soon immersed in her work, glancing only once at Ben, who was gazing out of the window across the autumn gardens, with a strange, bitter blankness in his eyes.

By lunchtime, China had practically finished her typing. She had worked at a furious pace all morning, never stopping for a moment and declining Ben's offer of coffee at eleven, with a vague inattentive shake of her head, not seeing the tender amusement on his face as he stared at the bent concentration of her head.

They lunched together in the kitchen. China ladled out huge bowls of thick savoury soup, which they ate with crusty bread and cheese, followed by fresh fruit and coffee.

She asked Ben questions about his business. He had worked hard after leaving university, travelling the world, building up his fortune and his empire of property. It seemed as though there was hardly a country in the world where he did not own vast areas of land.

It only took her an hour to finish the notes after lunch, then she was free to fix up the guest room, play with Fortune and wonder about dinner. Something special seemed in order for Ben's guests, she thought, as she made up the bed and placed fresh flowers in the room next to Ben's.

It was a busy afternoon because she had to drive into the village to purchase some fresh vegetables for the meal she was planning. She was pulling back into the drive when she saw a low red sports car in front of her: Ben's guests, no doubt, arriving early. She slowed down and allowed the distance to lengthen between the two cars, looking down at her old tight jeans and faded jumper with dismay. Perhaps she would be able to slip in the back way and keep a low profile until dinner.

Her plans were foiled by Ben, who was standing by the huge front door and who waved her towards him as soon as he saw her. Sighing, China pulled in behind the red sports car, and glanced miserably at herself in the rear view mirror. Her hair was snatched back into a manageable but hardly chic ponytail, her small face innocent of make-up, and this, coupled with the fact that her clothes had seen better days, left her in no mood to greet the visitors.

However, it seemed to be what Ben wanted, so grabbing her overflowing basket, she slid out of the car and walked gracefully towards the house.

Two people, a man and a woman, had emerged from the low red car, and as China approached Ben and the man were shaking hands, obviously very happy to see each other, obviously old and affectionate friends. She watched the warmth in Ben's dark face with an aching heart.

Then he turned to greet the elegantly-dressed woman who was waiting on the steps, and China saw his expression change as he bent to kiss the woman's cheek, a flicker of emotion in his eyes that she could not interpret, a very, very slight stiffening of his powerful body, something tenuous, but obvious to China as she looked on.

Ben noticed her then, his amber eyes skimming over her, missing nothing, as she stood alone, clutching the basket of vegetables in front of her as though it was a weapon.

'China, I'd like to introduce you to these very old and dear friends of mine, Olivia and Charles Daniels. Olivia, Charles, this is China Harmon.'

China smiled, murmuring polite greetings as Charles Daniels shook her hand, his dark eyes admiring on her finely-boned face. She did not notice because all her attention was fixed on Olivia Daniels and as soon as that lady spoke, China knew that she was the angry, possessive woman who had telephoned and left a message for Ben. Olivia had sounded more like an angry lover than a friend, and China was startled to find that she was married.

She held out her hand, noting the slight hesitation in the other woman, before she too held out a cool, limp hand for China's greeting.

'How do you do, Miss Harmon. I'm sorry, it is Miss, is it?' Low, honeyed tones laced with poison, China thought, taking a strong and instant dislike to Olivia Daniels.

'Hello, Mrs Daniels, and no, I'm not married,' she smiled, her voice bland and polite, as she looked at Ben's very old and very dear friend.

In her mid-thirties, Olivia Daniels was very beautiful, with stark, delicate features and opaque, skilfully made up eyes, her glinting dark brown hair neatly swept into a chignon that should have looked severe but in fact only served to emphasise the delicacy of her face.

She wore black, slim-fitting knickerbockers in a tweedy material with a fine wool sweater and a pale tweed jacket, delicate gold jewellery and long leather boots completing her outfit. She was cool, beautiful and sophisticated, everything that I'm not, China thought sadly.

Olivia Daniels turned away from her, making it clear that she had no interest in the younger girl, and slipped her arm possessively through Ben's. China watched with a kind of horrified fascination as she leaned forward and murmured something to him that neither China or Charles could hear. Ben smiled slightly, his eyes meeting China's, easily reading the faint shock he saw in her. He gently but firmly disengaged himself from Olivia Daniels and took China's basket from her. 'Come inside and have a drink. Charles, you and I can fetch the luggage later.'

Imagining that the invitation of a drink did not include her, China made her way to the kitchen, trying to concentrate on her dinner recipes, but finding that she was thinking about Ben and Olivia Daniels.

It was crystal clear that Mrs Daniels found Ben attractive; she had not even looked at her husband since they arrived. There was also the telephone message China had taken and that indefinable something that she had seen in Ben, when he had greeted the lovely older woman. Very strange. Perhaps, and the thought leapt unbidden into her mind, perhaps they were having an affair.

She sank into a chair, shocked at her own thoughts, and nearly stepped on Fortune, who was curled up beneath the seat. No, that was ridiculous, and she certainly had no evidence to substantiate such a suspicion.

However, the doubt would not be dispelled from her mind; it lingered, as though she had subconsciously picked up some vibrations between Ben and Olivia, nothing that she could put into words, just something vague, misty and infinitely depressing. The very thought of Ben and Olivia making love turned the blood in her veins to ice.

'Oh God,' she moaned aloud, 'this is *stupid* and I won't even think about it!'

'About what?' Ben's cool voice was behind her, and she turned in her seat to find him standing in the doorway, still idly holding the basket of vegetables in one hand.

China's heart beat faster at the sight of him, so tall and strong, filling the room with his presence.

'What won't you think about, China?' he asked again, still amused, as he strolled towards her and placed the basket on the table.

'N-Nothing. I was just thinking aloud,' she stammered, aware that her face was stained with guilty embarrassment.

Ben shrugged, lifting his wide shoulders uncaringly. 'You're such a secretive child,' he said softly, staring down at her with light flaring in his unfathomable golden eyes. 'Come and have a drink with us. I'd like you to get to know Olivia and Charles.'

'I'm not dressed,' China protested, hurt that he had called her a secretive child. He would not want to know her secrets anyway.

'Rubbish,' Ben said briskly. 'You look perfectly okay to me.' He took her hand and pulled her to her feet, casually sliding his arm around her slender shoulders and propelling her towards the door.

Being so close to him was almost unbearable, his casual, uncaring touch scalded her and she found it difficult to breathe, difficult to fight her almost overwhelming desire to go into his arms, to lift her mouth beggingly for his kiss.

But she walked beside him quietly and calmly, giving away none of her inner longings, feeling an

acid, unreasonable bitterness welling up in her heart.
He could manipulate her so easily.

'You always get your own way, don't you?' she
muttered bleakly, meeting his surprised glance with
defiance.

Ben's mouth twisted cynically. 'Don't you believe
it, sweetheart,' he replied cuttingly, destroying her
with a sudden harsh glance that held a dark significance that she did not understand.

'But I do believe it. I suppose it's because you're
so overbearing, so damned sure of yourself,' she
snapped, suddenly losing control of her temper.
She cared for him so very much and he would
never know, let alone reciprocate such caring. It
was very hard to bear, and she could not control
herself, even though she knew that her words were
unjust.

She saw his mouth tighten at her insult and his
arm dropped from her shoulder as though he could
no longer bear to touch her.

'What's the matter now?' he questioned in a
patient, deceptively calm voice.

China could have hit him. There was something
in his tight self-control that always made her lose
hers completely.

'I don't suppose it occurred to you that I may not
want a drink, that I may not want anything to do
with your friends,' she said with cold weariness,
admitting to herself that she did not want to have to
compete with Olivia Daniels.

Ben's eyes were hard and very angry. 'You're
right, that hadn't occurred to me. You're under no
obligation, of course.' He turned away and strode
towards the sitting-room.

China stood still for a second, appalled by her
own rudeness, then she ran after him, not question-

ing her actions, and laid her hand tentatively on his arm.

'Ben, I'm sorry—I was very rude. I would like a drink and I would like to know your friends,' she said quickly, her huge eyes beseeching his forgiveness.

He looked down at her, golden eyes probing, then he sighed, slipping his arm around her shoulder again and hugging her close to his body.

'I'm sorry too. I guess I tend to be dictatorial,' he smiled.

They entered the sitting-room together. Charles Daniels was at the window, sipping his drink in silence, his eyes distant as he gazed over the grounds of the house. Olivia sat by the fire, looking fragile and beautiful, her cold eyes narrowing on Ben's arm around China's shoulder. China sensed a certain tension between man and wife, as though they had been arguing before she and Ben had come in.

'What will you have?' Ben asked, smiling at her, sensing that she needed reassurance.

'Vodka and tonic, I think,' she answered, wanting something strong to calm the fluttering nerves in her stomach.

Ben lifted his dark brows but said nothing, handing her a glass, and pouring out a measure of whisky for himself.

They sat down, China opposite Olivia and Ben between them. Charles also sat down and chatted to China, deliberately trying to lighten the ominous atmosphere in the room.

Charles Daniels was a nice man, China decided, laughing at something he had said. He was witty and kind and lighthearted. Olivia was rather silent, prettily pleading a slight headache, but China felt her assessing eyes like knives.

'You're Ben's housekeeper, I take it. How long
have you been working for him?' she asked suddenly,
her beautiful red mouth curved into a sweet smile
that owed nothing to kindness.

China wondered if she was being deliberately patronising and decided that she was.

'Not very long, less than two weeks in fact,' she
answered quietly, meeting the older woman's eyes
with calm amusement.

Olivia raised her thin eyebrows.

'Cheaper than a wife, I suppose, Ben, my darling.
And she certainly looks as though she works hard.'
The green eyes skimmed dismissively over China's
untidy swathe of hair and old clothes.

Ben was silent, a slight smile curving his mouth,
his golden eyes blank and remote. China prayed that
he would defend her against the bitchy Mrs Daniels,
but no such defence was forthcoming. She felt drab
and dirty, and the innuendo behind Olivia's words
had not passed her by.

I wish I were his lover, she thought fiercely, unable
to keep the dislike out of her eyes as she glanced at the
other woman, because I think it would surprise and
anger you so much that you might leave here.

Avoiding Charles' sad, sympathetic eyes, she
finished her drink quickly, the last mouthful of raw
spirit making her choke, and was further humiliated
by Olivia Daniels' openly amused laughter at her
difficulty. She got to her feet, mustering the last
shreds of her dignity and excused herself in a toneless
voice, tired and uncaring what implications Ben
might read into her actions.

She prepared dinner carefully, making certain
that no derogatory comments could be passed about
the meal. She had decided on consommé, followed
by poached salmon in hollandaise sauce, served with

small, sweet peas, broccoli, asparagus and creamed
potato, followed by crêpes Suzettes and cheese.

She fervently wished that she had not agreed to
join Ben and his guests for dinner. He had asked her
while she was typing that morning and she had
agreed, not really listening to what he had been
saying. Stupid of me, she thought, rinsing the vegetables with careless violence.

As soon as the preparations were finished, she went
into her sitting-room and sat in front of the blazing
fire with Fortune on her lap, sighing with contentment as she looked around her.

It was dark outside, but she had not yet pulled
closed the velvet curtains. Outside, she could hear
the wind in the trees, and see the branches near the
windows waving. The room was bright and warm
and cosy.

She let her eyes rest on things lovingly—the bowl
of late flowers that she had picked the day before,
while walking with Fortune, a small ivory carving
that Clare had bought her for her birthday, and the
bright appliquéd cushions that she had made herself,
during her time in Italy. She had made this place
her own, her home, and when she had to leave it
would break her heart.

A sense of finality filled her and she felt depressed.
The arrival of Olivia Daniels had somehow made
her feel insecure, but worse than that, it had showed
her that she felt very deeply for Ben.

The thought of Olivia Daniels, or any other
woman for that matter, being his lover squeezed her
heart with a pain that could only be ascribed to jea-
lousy.

It was shocking and frightening, but it had to be
faced. She had fallen deeply and irrevocably in love
with Ben Galloway.

CHAPTER SIX

SHE sat perfectly still for at least twenty minutes letting the full implications of this self-revelation sink in. How could she love Ben? She had known him for such a short time and for most of that time she had disliked him intensely. Too intensely perhaps.

It was also clear that he did not love her, and that hurt. I ought to leave, she thought, glancing around the room and knowing that she wouldn't. Tears of self-pity gathered in her eyes. How could he have invaded and possessed her heart so carelessly? How could he have turned her life upside down and back to front without even trying? Damn him!

She got to her feet, putting a sleepy Fortune gently on to the rug. She would take a bath, a long hot bath, just the place to wallow in self-pity. As she ran the water, she considered what she would wear for dinner. She would look good, and the confidence such knowledge would give her, would, she hoped, help her to cope with Ben and Olivia Daniels.

She soaked in the hot, scented water for as long as she could, then shampooed her hair vigorously, unable to dispel thoughts of Ben from her mind.

As she stepped out of the bath, she glanced down at her naked body with dissatisfaction. Olivia Daniels was fashionably slender, while her own figure could only be described as curvaceous—full breasts, a narrow waist and rounded hips above long, shapely legs. Her skin was as white as alabaster and in her present mood of dissatisfaction, she longed to be tanned.

Sighing, she slipped into a twelling bathrobe and buttoned it quickly, combing out her wet hair in front of the mirror.

Her face was finely boned and pointed, with large, vividly blue eyes, a small nose and a gentle mouth. Not beautiful by any standards, she thought, pulling a face at herself, totally unaware of her own attraction.

She wandered into the sitting-room to dry her hair by the fire, sinking on to the floor to enjoy the warmth, so deep in thought that she did not hear the knock on the door, only looking up as Ben towered over her, holding two cups in his hands.

He looked very tired, she thought inconsequentially, his lean, beautiful face drawn and rather haggard. She smiled at him, her pale wet hair falling over her face.

'Hello,' she said softly.

Ben smiled back. 'Hi, I've brought you some coffee and I thought maybe I could join you,' he said, handing her a cup.

'You're welcome to.' She gestured to one of the comfortable chairs near the fire. 'And thanks for the coffee.'

Ben coiled himself into the chair with weary ease, watching her as she sat curled up at his feet, combing out her long hair. There was only one lamp switched on, a red, ceramic lamp that stood on the mantelpiece, bathing the two of them in soft light and leaving the rest of the room in partial darkness.

'Where are your guests?' China asked, staring at him from over the rim of her cup.

Ben laughed. 'Rowing in their room. I decided to keep out of the way.'

'Tell me about them—have you known them for years and years?'

'I've known Charles since I was at university. We

came together on the second day of the first term
and have been friends ever since. I remember he didn't
want to be at the university, but his parents wouldn't
allow him to go to art college. He's an architect now, in
great demand too. A compromise, I guess.' He sounded
quite sad as he talked about his friend.

'And Olivia?' China tried to keep her voice even,
surprised at her own daring in asking the question.

'I met Olivia when she married Charles, four years
ago. She was a top fashion model and Charles
pursued her relentlessly until she agreed to marry
him,' Ben said casually, as though Olivia meant
nothing to him. He was very convincing and China
almost believed him. He looked around the room, as
if he was bored with talking about Charles and
Olivia. 'You've given this room a calmness, a serenity that it never had before. I hope you don't mind
me coming here,' he said quietly.

'No, I'm glad you came,' she murmured honestly,
wishing that she could touch the hard bones of his
face. He seemed so alone. 'Ben . . .' She looked up
into his golden eyes, dry-mouthed and suddenly lost
for words.

Their glances locked and China could not keep
the hunger out of her eyes. Ben leaned forward,
reaching for her, whispering her name as his hands
closed on her shoulders. He pulled her near to him,
trapping her between the hard muscles of his thighs.

China lifted her mouth instinctively as she had
imagined doing so many times and his lips moved
over hers in small, hungry kisses that parted her lips,
clinging, breaking and clinging again, until at last,
with a groan that seemed to come from his very soul,
he pulled her against his hard chest, his kiss deep-
ening as he explored the inner softness of her mouth
with an urgency that made her cling to him.

'Hold me, China,' he whispered deeply, and sensing the need in him, driven by her love, she slid her arms around his waist, splaying her fingers across the broad sweep of his back, to hold him closer.

He was kissing her face now, closing her eyes with his mouth, trailing tiny kisses across her cheek, her chin, her slender throat, his fingers unbuttoning the neckline of her robe to allow his warm mouth access to the soft, scented skin of her shoulders.

China arched back her head, and a warm, sensual ache ran through her body at his touch. She was at the mercy of her love, her need for him, her heart pounding, defeaning her to all sensible, coherent thought.

Ben found her mouth again, his lips gentle, demanding and a tremor of pure sexual excitement shivered through her. The robe was open to her waist, exposing her full, soft breasts, and Ben stared down at her body, her white skin glimmering in the firelight, with glittering eyes. He drew a long, harsh breath.

'You're so beautiful,' he murmured huskily, his eyes flaming with desire and a gentleness that stopped her heart. He kissed her throat, his hands closing over her breasts to slowly and possessively caress, his long tanned fingers stroking over her nipples in the most intimate and delicate caress she had ever known.

'China, I need you,' he groaned, against the pulse that beat frantically in her throat, and she shuddered, matching his need with her own need to satisfy him.

With shy, trembling fingers she fumbled with the buttons of his shirt, finally feeling the hard, rough warmth of his chest beneath her hands. She touched him shyly, making him draw breath unevenly, tangling her fingers in the mat of dark hair that covered his chest, feeling his heartbeat racing away, pounding as fast as her own.

He pulled her back into his arms suddenly, and their bodies came together for the first time. She felt the wonderful warmth of his skin against her naked breasts. He held her so tightly that she could hardly breathe.

'China, let me love you. You've haunted me ever since that first day. . . .'

She stopped him with her mouth, letting her fingers roam over the smooth tanned skin of his powerful shoulders. She wanted him badly. He was the only man she would ever want and he would be a strong, gentle lover, who would teach her things she could not even dream about. He was waiting for her answer, not pushing her, still holding her tightly. I love him, she thought fiercely, at the mercy of her emotions.

The telephone began to ring, demanding an answer, loud and insistent, breaking into the spell that wound around them.

'Ben. . . .' China did not want him to move. As far as she was concerned, it could ring for ever.

He smiled at her, his eyes tender, and got to his feet, cursing under his breath. She sat watching him, watching his easy catlike grace as he walked into her bedroom to answer the telephone.

A moment later he was at her side again, his eyes dark on her body.

'James,' he said bleakly, his mouth angry and abrupt.

'Ben, please. . . .' she began.

'I'm sorry, China,' he said harshly, and strode from the room, slamming the door violently behind him.

She struggled to her feet, still lethargic with desire,

and buttoned her robe with hasty, trembling fingers,
feeling so lonely and abandoned that she wanted to
cry. Oh, Ben! Her heart was an aching stone inside
her chest.

James was very bright and very cheerful, asking
her out to dinner the following night, persuading
her by saying that he did not know how long he
would be in England. She agreed provisionally, explaining that she would have to check with Ben. She
felt sure in her own mind, though, that he would have
no objection. He would probably be glad to get rid of
her for an evening, she thought desperately, flicking
away a tear that had rolled down on to her cheek.

She tried to be as bright as James as she spoke to
him, but she did not succeed. He sounded concerned,
but did not press her to tell him what was wrong.

She dressed slowly for dinner, setting her hair
before applying her make-up carefully. She used more
eye make-up than usual, stroking her eyelids with a
silvery shadow and darkening her lashes with mascara,
finally colouring her mouth with rich soft colour.

Then she dressed in a white silk dress that had a
simple, clinging style and very pale blue flowers
along its hem. With the silver pendant around her
neck and pale blue high-heeled sandals completing
her outfit, she brushed out her hair, letting it fall in
soft gleaming waves around her shoulders.

She was ready, and examining herself in one of
the full-length mirrors in her bedroom, she was very
pleased with the result of all her effort. She looked
poised, and sophisticated, almost pretty, the armour
she needed to face an evening in the company of the
bitchy Olivia Daniels.

She walked through into the kitchen and checked
the meal, which was cooking satisfactorily, then into
the dining-room to set the table. She could hear

Olivia Daniels' tinkling laughter coming from the sitting room, and grimaced. No doubt Ben would be keeping her amused, China thought bitterly, slamming shut the drawer that contained the cutlery.

With everything under control, she had five minutes to herself when the table was finished. She plucked a cigarette from the ornate jade box on the table and lit it, drawing the smoke deep into her lungs and wandered over to the window. The moon was almost full in a clear cold sky, a foretaste of winter.

What shall I do? she wondered. If I stay here, loving Ben the way I do, it will break my heart.

A hand placed lightly on her shoulder made her jump, her shining head spinning round. Ben stood beside her, as though brought to her by the telepathy of her thoughts.

'Are you all right?' he asked softly, turning her to face him in the light, his fierce, lion eyes searching her face.

China looked at him in silence, feeling a faint spark of resentment inside herself that he could make her love him, without even trying.

He had changed for dinner. His thick dark hair was faintly damp from the shower and he wore a white dinner jacket, startling against his tanned skin, expensively tailored to his muscular body, and dark trousers. He was so near to her that she could breathe in the faint, clean male scent of his skin, and her heart began to beat faster.

'Of course I'm all right,' she replied, sounding vaguely scornful. 'What did you expect, that I'd break up after being in your arms?' She stared at him defiantly, an uncharacteristically cold smile curving her mouth.

The gentleness faded from Ben's eyes, to be

replaced by the blank hard look she was accustomed to, and she also felt the slight tensing of his body. He must never know how he could affect her. She meant nothing to him, but if he ever found out how she loved him, she would not even be left with her pride.

'No, I didn't expect you to break up,' he said expressionlessly, his fingers tightening fractionally on her shoulders. 'I've learned to expect nothing from you.' His words cut into her like knives even though she knew that she had brought this hurt on herself. She struggled in his grasp, trying to prise his steel-strong fingers from her shoulders, angry tears flashing in her eyes.

'Take your hands off me, your touch makes my flesh creep!' she spat at him, so hurt and angry that she was hardly aware of what she was saying, only knowing her need to retaliate.

He did not let her go, but stared down at her with cold, angry eyes, and behind the anger there was something else, a flash of emotion that, had she not known him better, she might have interpreted as pain.

'Then you're a very good actress, my love. I could have sworn your response was genuine,' he murmured in a soft, deadly voice.

'You were wrong—I hate you!' China managed through clenched teeth, fighting the desire that he induced merely by his nearness.

Ben's dark brows lifted. 'I know, and you can't bear my touch. Quite a transformation, and I might believe you except that I've tasted your response, your mouth, your soft white skin. You can't pretend it didn't happen, China, it's branded on my memory.' His voice was a soft drawl and her face burned with humiliation at his words.

'Ben, I . . . you. . . .' Her voice trailed off as she looked at the compressed violence of his mouth.

'God knows I should have taken you, possessed your beautiful white body when I had the chance,' he said darkly, his eyes flaring with raw, hungry desire.

'You wouldn't have got the chance,' she retorted heatedly.

Ben smiled thinly. 'You wouldn't have stopped me—you didn't stop me. You wanted me, darling, almost as badly as I wanted you.' His gaze was openly insolent on her body, as though he could see through the white silk to her nakedness below.

China hung her head in silence. There was nothing to say. He was speaking the truth, no matter how much that hurt. She could not lie. Ben sighed heavily and released her, as though he was terribly weary of fighting. He lit a cigarette and drew on it deeply, seating himself on the edge of the table, watching her with remote, unreadable eyes as he allowed his anger to visibly drain away.

China knew that now was her chance to get away, to leave the room, but she found that she did not want to move. She watched him smoking, watched his obvious effort to rid himself of his anger, captivated by his strength, his masculine beauty, overwhelmed by the depth of her love for him. He smiled at her suddenly. 'I'm sorry,' he said simply. 'I don't know what it is with us, sparks fly with every contact. Can I take you out to dinner tomorrow night?' He saw the bewilderment in her eyes and added. 'There's no ulterior motive, child, no strings attached, just dinner. A new start.'

China longed to say yes. It was what they needed, a new start, that would perhaps sort out the mess between them. Then she remembered James; she had already promised to have dinner with him.

'I'm sorry, I can't,' she said quietly, feeling as though she was letting something pure and precious slip through her fingers into the dirt.

'Why not? Tell me, China, I'm entitled to know.'

'I'm having dinner with James,' she explained, wondering why the thought of it sounded so dull.

'I see.' Ben's voice was bitter, his anger barely controlled, as he stubbed out his cigarette with violent fingers.

China opened her mouth to explain, to ask about another evening, but he cut across her before she had time to speak.

'For God's sake, spare me the details, no explanations are necessary,' he muttered, and left the room.

As far as China was concerned dinner was a disaster, although the actual food was delicious. She found that she had no appetite at all, barely managing a few choking mouthfuls of soup, and pushing her salmon around the plate until it looked quite revolting and definitely inedible. It was quite a relief to be able to get up and down from her seat, to attend to the serving of the food.

Olivia Daniels looked very beautiful in a black crêpe dress adorned with diamond and gold jewellery. She chatted to Ben over the meal, barely acknowledging the presence of her husband, which China found appalling. Seated opposite to Ben, China could observe him as Olivia demanded his attention. He was charming and polite, but she could read the tightness of his mouth even if she could not read his inscrutable amber eyes.

She chatted to Charles, glad to be able to divert his attention from his wife's obvious behaviour. They were talking about fishing, when a loud comment by Olivia cut across their chatter.

'Such a novel idea, having the paid help sitting down to dinner—you're quite a liberal at heart, Ben my love.'

There was an ominous silence and China flushed scarlet with embarrassment, wishing that she could disappear. Ben was staring at her with cool, distant eyes, seemingly unconcerned with what was going on at his dinner table.

'Mind your tongue, Olivia!' Charles snapped angrily into the silence, his face quite red, as he defended China.

Olivia laughed without amusement, her eyes malicious and slightly fevered as they rested on her husband.

'One can always rely on Charles to support the underdog,' she said with mild but obvious sarcasm.

Charles stiffened, his face becoming redder as he tried to control his fury. 'I won't tell you again, Olivia,' he warned angrily.

'Oh, Charles, you really are amusing,' she mocked in reply, knowing how to hit for the maximum effect.

China pressed a trembling hand to her mouth, her fork clattering on to the table, her face ashen. She despised scenes, especially those where people were trying to destroy each other.

Ben glanced at her, his eyes darkening on her small, frightened face.

'Olivia, I think it would be a good idea if you went to your room,' he said slowly and commandingly.

Olivia turned to face him, a sharp retort hovering on her lips, but his face was dark and arrogant and brooked no argument. Casting China and Charles poisonous, febrile looks, she got to her feet and flounced from the room, slamming the door behind her.

'Ben, I don't know what to say,' Charles said uneasily. He turned to China. 'I can only apologise for Olivia's dreadful behaviour.'

China managed a shaky smile. 'It's not your fault,' she said, trying to put him at ease, shocked by the naked pain and embarrassment in his face.

'Perhaps you could take Olivia some coffee,' Ben suggested gently to his friend.

Charles jumped to his feet at once, obviously glad of an excuse to leave the room.

China kept her head down when he had gone, sipping her coffee quickly, even though it was too hot, anxious to get away herself. She knew that Ben was watching her.

'Poor little China,' he taunted softly. 'Your lovely meal wasted.'

She glared at him. 'It doesn't matter,' she said stiffly.

Ben smiled. 'Did that sordid little scene upset you?'

'I certainly didn't find it as amusing as you obviously did,' she retorted.

'Their marriage is on the rocks,' Ben stated flatly. He did not seem to care. Perhaps he was waiting for Olivia to be free. She frowned.

'Olivia has a poisonous tongue, don't let her upset you,' he said, in a curiously strange tone.

'I won't,' China replied in a small voice.

'I'm glad to hear it. You're no match for her, she's had plenty of practice, sharpening her claws on young innocents like you. You were being kind to Charles and she didn't like it.' Ben's eyes narrowed shrewdly on her face.

'But she doesn't want him,' China mused, her face puzzled. 'Why should she care if I talk to him?'

'You're young and you're very lovely, two very good reasons,' Ben drawled softly.

'I still don't understand,' China said, her senses still reeling from his husky compliments. There seemed no logic in what he was saying.

'Forget it,' he advised, suddenly harsh. 'Perhaps all this will serve as a warning, just in case you've got your sights set on my dear brother.'

'You swine!' she muttered, hating him.

His wide shoulders lifted eloquently. 'Love turned sour is always painful. You still have that lesson to learn,' he said uncaringly.

And what would you know about love? she wanted to scream at him, but of course she didn't, she got to her feet and began to clear away the dishes.

Charles helped her to wash up, profusely apologetic about the incident over dinner.

'Both Olivia and I have known for a long time that our marriage is over, it's difficult to give in gracefully,' he said, drying a plate with fast efficiency.

'Do you still love her?' China asked, sensing his sadness.

'I don't know. A relationship with Olivia is rather like becoming hooked on drugs. It's a habit that I need.'

'I'm so sorry,' she mumbled, feeling very miserable for him. He seemed rather desperate. 'What will you do?'

'She wants a divorce, and I agree that it's the best thing under the circumstances,' Charles replied broodingly. 'I'm only sorry that you had to be dragged into this damnable mess.'

'Don't worry, damnable messes are becoming my speciality,' China laughed wryly, and they finished the work in friendly harmony.

She did not want to face Ben again, so she slipped
off to her room as soon as the kitchen was cleared
up, apologising to Charles and pleading a headache.
He seemed to understand.

Once in the sanctuary of her room, however, she
felt strangely restless and unable to sit down for more
than a moment at a time. She was full of energy, no
doubt born of frustration. I need some exercise, she
thought ruefully, glancing out of the window. It was
far too dark and cold for a walk. Then she remembered the swimming pool. Ben had given her
permission to use it at any time and she had a
swimming costume that she had bought in Italy. It
was the perfect solution, a few lengths of rigorous
swimming would tire her out sufficiently before bed,
and she might even be able to sleep.

She ran into her bedroom and searched through
the chest of drawers for her costume, then grabbing
her towelling robe, made her way to the pool. A
sense of forbidden excitement filled her, as though
she was disobeying some unwritten law of etiquette
by swimming at midnight.

She reached the conservatory without bumping
into Ben or Olivia or Charles, which was a relief,
and switched on just one of the overhead lights, the
one directly over the pool.

She smiled to herself in secret pleasure at such
lovely solitude, then quickly changed into her black
bikini, and standing on the edge of the pool, per-
formed a graceful swallow dive into the artificially
warm water.

She gasped as she surfaced, the water seeming cold
against her heated skin, but it only took a few
seconds to become used to it, and she splashed
around like a contented child.

It was heaven! She floated on to her back, staring

up at the stars outside, through the exotic greenery of the huge tropical plants that filled the glass room, and thought of Ben, her heart contracting with love for him.

She would have to leave Aspenmere Hall soon, and the knowledge weighed her down with sadness. She swam up and down the pool as fast as she could, in an effort to wear herself out. She really would have to get a good night's sleep, she was beginning to look and feel dreadful. Perhaps I ought to get drunk, she thought amusedly, and laughed out loud to herself.

She suddenly felt lightheaded and, for some inexplicable reason, rather happy. She was in love for the first time in her life, and what did they say? Better to have loved and lost. She would lose Ben Galloway, but she would love him for ever, and at this time of night it did not seem to matter.

She caught sight of him a moment later, standing by the door of the conservatory, idly smoking, his white jacket slung casually over his shoulder. He was watching her with veiled eyes.

He probably thinks I'm a lunatic, swimming and laughing to myself at this time of night, she thought, feeling the inevitable racing of her pulses at the sight of him.

'What are you doing here?' she called, floating on to her back again and kicking up a fountain of water.

'I was walking in the garden and saw the light,' he replied, strolling indolently to the edge of the pool.

'Come and swim with me,' she invited, feeling the madness in her blood.

He smiled. 'Don't you want to be alone?'

'No, I didn't come here to be alone, just to swim

for a while.' China tried to explain. 'The water is very warm—lovely,' she encouraged.

Moments later Ben dived cleanly into the pool and swam towards her. He was a powerful swimmer, his muscular brown body cutting through the water with ease and speed.

'You look happy,' he remarked, surfacing beside her.

Her breath caught painfully in her throat as she looked at him, water falling from his broad, naked shoulders in diamond drops.

'I'm happy because I don't care any more,' she laughed, her eyes brilliantly reckless as she stared up into his dark face.

'Lucky you,' he said, his mouth twisting wearily. He seemed mesmerised by her brightness, unable to take his eyes off her. 'China, I want to talk to you.' His voice was low and serious, and she turned away in panic.

'Don't be serious, Ben—not tonight,' she begged, feeling absurdly close to tears, almost hysterical. 'I couldn't bear it.' She moved to swim away, but he caught her arm, pulling her effortlessly towards him.

'You'll have to bear it,' he muttered, his amber eyes irritated.

'No,' she whispered, her hands moving to his bare brown shoulders in an effort to steady herself in the water. 'Kiss me instead.' The words were out before she realised, expressing her deepest longings. But before she had time to retract them, he had drawn her into his arms, his mouth finding hers with unerring precision, kissing her with cool, urgent lips, as his hands slid the length of her wet, half-naked body, from throat to thigh.

China clung to him, returning his kiss with innocent passion, her own hands curling against his smooth, tense back.

Sudden fear of self-betrayal made her twist away from him, seconds later, and he let her go easily, not attempting to take her back into his arms.

She stared at him with huge, bruised eyes and he touched her mouth gently with a lean forefinger.

'Don't look so stricken, child. You invited that kiss,' he mocked wickedly, not looking at all repentant.

'I know—silly of me, I suppose,' she laughed, unable to comprehend the lightning changes in her emotions, her moods.

He stared at her broodingly for a second, then said, 'Olivia and Charles will be leaving tomorrow. I think they both realise that their visit here was a disastrous idea, and Charles is very embarrassed about the shabby way Olivia's treated you.'

'It doesn't matter,' China cut in quickly. 'He's your friend, and I don't want him to feel that he has to leave because of me.'

Ben smiled gently. 'I know.' He paused, then said, 'It would be very easy for Charles to fall in love with you.'

He surprised her and she lifted puzzled eyes to his face. 'I don't understand.'

'Don't you? Are you really so unworldly that you don't know the effect you have on men?' he asked, his mouth compressing wryly.

China frowned. 'Are you making fun of me?' she queried painfully.

'Oh, China!' Ben sighed gently, half laughing, half groaning. 'You're always so defensive.' He stroked her wet hair away from her face in a soft, sensual movement. 'Charles took one look at you, at your beauty, at your kindness, and he couldn't drag his eyes away. Your generous heart burns from within, illuminating you, a warm beacon in a barren landscape for men like him.'

China flushed, embarrassed and joyful from his compliments. 'I'm sure you're talking rubbish,' she said, trying to keep her tone light.

'I think you know that I'm not. Tell me about James,' Ben said expressionlessly.

Startled by the abrupt change of subject, she stared at him, trying to read the expression in his narrowed eyes. There was nothing to tell about James, her heart was filled with Ben.

'I'm very fond of him,' she said cautiously, after a slight pause.

'Fond?' He threw the word back at her insultingly. 'What sort of weak emotion is that?' he jibed, and she sensed a sudden flash of anger in him. Defiance filled her. If she was not careful, he would trick her into admitting her love for him. He was far too clever.

'I don't think it's any of your business,' she said coldly.

'That's where you're wrong. I've made it my business. Tell me, China, is it thoughts of James that give you that faraway dreamy look I catch in your eyes, whenever you think you're alone?' His voice was contemptuous, laced with anger, his hands were cruel on her shoulders, as they stood together in the warm water, with the October wind howling outside the thick glass walls of the conservatory.

She paled visibly at such perception. Was she so easy to read? Did he already know of her love for him?

'What if it is?' she muttered defensively, not quite lying but not telling him the truth either. 'You don't even know what love is!' she added spitefully, hitting back at him for hurting her so easily.

Ben laughed, cold humourless laughter. 'At least we're getting to the truth. Love is decidedly more positive than fond, wouldn't you agree?'

His voice was dark, and she realised that he had misunderstood her. He thought she loved James, which meant that he had no idea of her love for him, and also would keep him from guessing the truth.

'You're hurting me!' she protested. His long fingers had tightened unbearably on her shoulders as though he wanted to snap her fragile bones.

'I'd like to kill you,' he said flatly, his voice totally devoid of expression, but he released her immediately.

China gazed into his dark, twisted face, feeling a little frightened, watching the evidence of some fierce inner battle raging within him.

'Why?' she whispered simply, shocked to the core by his violence.

'Even you are not that naïve,' Ben muttered, coldly and cryptically. He lifted his hand and raked it through his gleaming hair in a gesture of intense weariness.

China shook her head, totally lost, unable to drag her hungry eyes away from the powerful, graceful movements of his body.

'You're mad,' she stated, quite matter-of-factly.

'I think you're right,' he smiled sourly. 'By the way, I'm going away tomorrow. My flight leaves late in the afternoon.'

The news hit her like a blow in the stomach, and he sounded so damned casual.

'Away? Where to? For how long?' she questioned faintly, speaking her thoughts aloud.

'Why so shocked? Will you miss me, China?' He

was not serious, but she perceived a stillness in him, as though her answer was somehow important to him.

'Miss a slave-driver like you? Hardly.' She tried to joke, terrified of revealing her true feelings, but failed, miserably, only managing to sound insulting.

The stark bones of his face tightened as his jaw clenched, his eyes hard and brilliant as he stared at her, but he said nothing.

She swallowed convulsively, almost aching to beg him not to leave her.

'Is it business?' Her voice was very small and dry.

'Yes,' he replied smoothly. 'And as you're obviously so interested, I'll tell you. I'm going to Egypt, there's a big land deal on offer and I intend to get it,' he said briefly. 'Satisfied?'

'Will it take long?'

He shrugged. 'A month or so, I imagine, maybe longer. Why the sudden concern? I'd have thought you'd be glad to see the back of me. Are you planning to get James in while I'm away?' he queried sardonically.

'I have to know because of telephone calls and food and things like that. . . .' she said lamely, feeling so numb and miserable that she could hardly make her mouth form the words.

'Don't worry, I'll give you fair warning of my return, so that you can get rid of your lover—and as for the telephone, I'll leave instructions for that before I go.' Ben swam to the edge of the pool and levered himself out of the water.

China closed her eyes. She did not want him to go, not like this, with all this bitterness between them. She spoke his name softly and he turned to look at her. There was a tiredness about him that touched her heart.

'What is it?' His tone was final and uncompromising. It was no good.

'N-nothing . . . I'm sorry.' She turned away from him and began to swim the length of the pool. There was so much left hanging between them, so much left unsaid and misunderstood. She reached the far corner of the pool and turned back, wanting to talk to him, wanting to try again. She was alone. Ben had gone, and she let her tears run unchecked, down her face.

It was difficult to sleep that night even though she felt physically exhausted after all her swimming. Ben was going away for weeks and weeks and she did not know if she could bear it. She felt totally out of her depth; the situation was a disaster that left her nerves and her emotions twisted as tight as wire.

Ben thought she was in love with James—it was almost funny in a deadly, humourless way. I *must* get away from here, she thought desperately, as she at last drifted into a light, troubled sleep.

She was woken at seven by the alarm, feeling so worn out and depressed that even a brisk shower had no effect on her. She strolled into the kitchen, dragging lethargic feet, after dressing, and switched on the percolater.

It had been arranged the night before that she would take up a tray of coffee for Ben's guests, at seven-thirty. She made up two trays, one for Olivia and Charles and one for Ben, with slow, listless hands. The joys of being a housekeeper, she thought dully, opening the side door to let Fortune out into the garden.

While she was waiting for the coffee to brew, she plaited her long hair and secured it with an elastic band, looking down at her old jeans and ancient sweater with dissatisfaction, but no inclination to change into something smarter. She was in no mood to worry about her appearance, not today, the day when Ben would go away.

The coffee was ready. She filled two porcelain jugs from the percolater, deciding to take up Olivia and Charles' tray first.

She ran up the main stairs, carefully balancing the laden tray, stopping dead in her tracks as she reached Ben's room. The door was opening and Olivia Daniels emerged from inside, her rich hair tousled, her hands tightening the belt of her apricot-coloured silk and lace peignoir. There was a strange, frenzied look on her face that changed to a smug, satisfied smile, that lit her ravishing face with warmth as she saw China, clutching the tray.

'Ah, coffee,' Olivia said in a low cool, slightly-breathless voice, and taking the tray from China's numb fingers, without a word of thanks, opened the door of her own room and disappeared inside.

China swayed back against the carved banister, feeling physically sick. It was patently obvious what had been happening. Olivia Daniels had spent the night with Ben, while her husband, Ben's dear friend, had slept alone in the room next door. They were lovers, and China's worst suspicions were confirmed. She pressed a trembling hand to her mouth in anguish and dismay, her whole body shaking from head to foot.

How could Ben have kissed her so passionately last night, knowing that he would be spending the night in his lover's arms?

She ran downstairs like the wind, her eyes blind with tears, her heart frozen with despair, wondering how on earth she could love such a cold, heartless man.

CHAPTER SEVEN

THREE weeks and a few days later, China stepped off the plane at Athens airport, the heat hitting her like a tangible force as she made her way across the tarmac with the other passengers towards the airport buildings.

She looked round for James, but saw no sign of him. She hoped that he remembered that she was arriving today, the thought of struggling with all her luggage and finding a taxi to take her to the hotel did not appeal to her. But as she went through Immigration and Passport Control, she saw him waiting for her, waving brightly as he caught sight of her. She smiled back and as soon as all her papers had been checked, stamped and passed, she rushed over to him, so glad to see his friendly face again.

'You remembered!' she greeted him, laughingly.

'Of course I did.' He gave her a brotherly kiss on the cheek and a thorough scrutiny. 'You look thin,' he commented bluntly.

'I don't think so,' she replied untruthfully, knowing that she had lost weight over the past few weeks.

James shrugged. 'Let me take your luggage and then I'll show you the hotel.' Never one to waste time on unnecessary pleasantries, he picked up her two suitcases and led her outside to an open white sports car, stowing them in the boot and ushering her into the front passenger seat.

'How are you, James?' she asked, as the car pulled on to the main road and away from the low airport buildings.

'Fine, never better, and shall I tell you a secret? I'm in love,' he revealed happily, taking his eyes off the road to flash her a boyish smile.

China was a little surprised, but very happy for him.

'I'm very glad for you, anybody I know? Is she Greek?'

James shook his head. 'No, not Greek, and you may know her, but I can't talk about it at the moment, not even to you, sweet China, so I'm not going to tell you anything, apart from the fact that she's very beautiful and I'm sure you'll like her.'

'I'm sure I will,' China laughed. 'My curiosity is roused now, you secretive devil! When will I meet her?'

'I don't know—soon, I hope,' James replied cryptically.

'This is all very sudden, you know,' China began, fixing him with a mock-suspicious glare.

'You won't get round me like that,' James laughed. 'I shouldn't really have mentioned it, but I was bursting to tell somebody. And how about you? How are you? Tell me everything that's been happening to you since we last met. Why are you so pale and thin?'

The questions tumbled from his lips, questions that she could not answer.

'I'm fine, and nothing in particular has been happening to me—and it's not very gallant of you to say that I'm looking pale and thin!'

'Sorry, love, but I'm concerned about you. How's Ben?'

China swallowed convulsively. Even the casual mention of his name made her hurt inside.

'Fine, I imagine. I haven't seen him, he's away in Egypt,' she said quickly, hoping that her voice wasn't giving anything away.

'How did he take it—you throwing up the job, I mean?' James asked casually.

China flushed brightly, glad that James had to keep his eyes and his attention on the road.

'He wasn't pleased, but there was nothing he could do.' That was a downright lie, of course. She was not even certain that Ben knew yet, but she could not tell James that. She thought about the note she had left and cringed at her own cowardice.

When they reached the centre of Athens the car pulled off the main wide road into a smaller, tree-lined street, and screeched to a halt.

'This is it.' James jumped out and walked round to open the door. They stood outside a medium sized hotel, modern and attractive-looking, with a huge, exotic garden in front, scattered with white wrought iron tables, shaded by brightly coloured parasols, and surrounded by matching chairs.

James took her arm and they strolled through the garden and through the smoked glass doors into the reception area. It was quiet and deserted and rather eerie.

'It's all been redecorated,' he said proudly, and China looked around with interest.

By the time she had seen over the whole place she was hot, thirsty and quite dizzy, definitely unable to take everything in, but not wanting to squash James' pride and happiness.

He must have sensed her feelings, because looking at her, he suddenly clapped his hand to his forehead. 'Good God, I'm sorry! You must be dying for a drink after all that travelling, and I haven't even let you sit down. I just let my enthusiasm run away with me sometimes.' He apologised profusely and took her up to the top floor, where the apartments were situated. He led her into a comfortable lounge, furnished with bright, light, modern furniture.

'What would you like?' he asked.

'A cup of tea and a sandwich please,' China replied promptly, her stomach protesting loudly at the mere mention of food, as she strolled over to the large window.

'Your wish is my command. I'll only be a minute, make yourself at home.' He was gone before she could answer, making her smile. He was so different from Ben.

A plane went by overhead, low and loud, and she glanced out of the window, over the city, at the traffic, at the haze of heat that distorted everything, and she suddenly felt very lonely. What am I doing here? she asked herself. Have I really come all this way, just to get away from Ben?

She felt perilously near to tears, thankful that James reappeared at that moment with a tray in his hands, to divert her attention.

She drank her tea and managed most of her sandwich, although her thoughts of Ben had robbed her of her appetite, and let James talk.

'I'm so glad that you could come over for a holiday to see the place, before you make your decision,' he said, pouring out another cup of tea for her.

'So am I. It's good to see you again,' she replied, trying to make her voice sound normal. 'When will you open?' The hotel was safe ground for conversation and she could talk about it fairly easily.

'In about a month's time. Saul, my partner, is in the States at the moment, he'll be back in about a fortnight, then we'll have two weeks for the final preparations, so you've got plenty of time to make up your mind,' he said persuasively.

China smiled and finished her tea. Working here

might be her only option, but she did not intend to make a quick decision as she had with her last two jobs.

She got to her feet, gracefully tired. 'James, would you mind if I rested for a while? I feel exhausted after all that travelling.'

He nodded, jumping to his feet.

'I'll show you your rooms.' He led her to one of the apartments on the same floor and left her, promising to see her for dinner.

China walked into the bedroom. The slatted wooden shutters on the windows were closed and the room was blissfully cool. She took a quick shower, revelling in the coldness of the water on her dusty, overheated body, and slipped on a loose cotton caftan, marvelling at the heat. A couple of hours before she had been shivering in the cold English rain.

She lay down on the bed in the dim bedroom and despite trying not to, thought about what had happened at Aspenmere Hall.

After finding Olivia coming from Ben's bedroom, she had needed to get out of the house, unable to stay there a moment longer. She had grabbed the nearest coat and run from the house as though she had demons behind her.

Across the garden and into the winter trees, out of breath and choking with tears, she had thought that the pain in her heart would kill her. She had wandered through the woods for hours, her mind whirling with chaotic thoughts, unaware of the time, only forced back to the house by a violent cloudburst.

Ben had been furiously angry when she got back. It was after twelve and Olivia and Charles had already gone.

'Where the hell have you been?' he had demanded furiously, eyeing her trembling, soaking body with hard eyes.

Her pulses had raced at the sight of him, and she had cursed the treacherous weakness of her body, amazed at her response to him even when she was so hurt. He had always drawn her against her will, and that was the trouble with love, it did not disappear at convenient moments. It was there for ever.

'Out.' She had replied succinctly, her eyes resting on his tightly compressed mouth.

'You're paid to be here when I need you,' he had snapped, obviously having difficulty controlling his temper. 'If Mrs Stephenson hadn't come in. . . .'

'If you're not satisfied, why don't you sack me?' she had cut in wearily.

Ben had taken her arm then, sensing the numb coldness, the lack of caring in her.

'What is it? Are you sick?' His concern had made her feel worse, as though he had tricked her somehow.

'I'm sick of you,' she had retorted wildly. 'Why don't you leave me alone? If you want me to go, I'll go, but make up your mind.'

He had let her go, knowing that she would tell him nothing, and she had locked herself in her room for the rest of the day.

Even now, she could still not believe he was the sort of man who would have an affair with his best friend's wife. He was just like all the other men, like Signor Cencelli. She had thought him special, had even hoped that one day he might love her. What a joke!

She had seen Ben briefly before he left for the airport; he had insisted upon it. She had put on a false, bright face, frightened that he might change his plans if she stayed in her room and refused to see him.

She had been very convincing, apologising and blaming her earlier behaviour on illness, something she had eaten.

Ben had accepted it after a while, giving her instructions and promising to telephone. China had smiled at him, talked to him, acted so normally that she feared she was going insane, and all the time pain had been tearing inside her at the knowledge that she would not see him again, because she intended to be well gone from Aspenmere Hall by the time he returned from Egypt.

He had wanted to kiss her, touch her, hold her, she knew, but she deliberately warded off any suggestion of physical contact, until he got the message, and his beautiful mouth tightened, the rest of their conversation being short and to the point.

Then he had gone, in angry silence, and China had thought her heart would break as his car pulled down the drive. She had cancelled her dinner date with James and spent the rest of the day lying on her bed, staring at her painting and thinking.

Her arrangements for leaving Aspenmere Hall had been surprisingly simple. James had flown to Athens the week after Ben left and China had telephoned him there, asking about the job he had once offered. He had been pleased and surprised and, without asking questions, had formed plans for China to take this holiday to look over the place.

She had packed her belongings into boxes and tea chests, and left them, together with Fortune, in Mrs Stephenon's capable hands, until she returned. She typed out a brief note of resignation for Ben and looked around the house before she left. She had come to love Aspenmere Hall, she realised, and there was no trace left that she had ever been there. It was sad.

She knew that it was cowardly and underhand to sneak away while Ben was abroad, but it seemed the only thing to do under the circumstances. She was frightened by her love for him, it left her too vulnerable and open to being hurt. He did not love her, he probably loved Olivia Daniels, and knowing this, she could not possibly live under the same roof, seeing him every day. It was pointless self-destruction, so now she was here in Athens, thousands of miles away from Ben and Aspenmere Hall, but it didn't make it any easier, it didn't make it any easier at all.

She dressed listlessly for dinner, not feeling very hungry but knowing that she had to make the effort for James' sake. She made her face up, then slipped into a pale green cotton dress, cut in a gypsy style with a matching jacket, and left her hair loose, pinning it back from her face with two jade combs.

It was a very warm evening and looking out of her bedroom window, as she fastened a jade bracelet around her wrist, she saw that the city below her was coming to life. Perhaps life here will be an adventure, she thought hopefully, trying to dispel the depression that hung over her.

James met her at the lift. He too had changed into a pale linen suit and dark open-necked shirt. He drove her to a restaurant on the other side of the city where they ate fish and rice and peppers followed by fresh figs and washed down with ouzo and water, and thick, sweet coffee.

China found that her appetite had returned a little, and James tried hard to make her laugh. The ouzo helped too. The pleasant aniseed taste made it easy to drink, and she did not realise how strong it was, until she found herself giggling uncontrollably at something James had said, something not particularly funny at that.

He talked with endless enthusiasm about his plans for the hotel, and China listened carefully.

'If I take the job you're offering, what exactly will I be doing?' she asked, finding that the thought of working in Athens for a while, was beginning to sound more and more appealing.

James laughed, 'You may well ask! It would be a sort of all-round job. There would be secretarial work, supervision of staff, bookings, just about everything to do with running the hotel.'

'A big job,' China commented, sipping her coffee and finding the rich, sweet flavour to her taste.

'Well—yes. It would probably be round the clock to start off with, until we get the place on its feet, but you'd be well paid and one of the apartments on the top floor would be yours. I need somebody who I know will work hard, somebody I can trust, and preferably a friend, like you,' he finished charmingly.

'I'll think seriously about it,' China promised. She had to admit that it sounded ideal. She could lose herself in a job like that, never having a moment free to brood about Ben. It was exactly what she needed, so why was she hesitating about committing herself?

She excused herself as soon as they got back to the hotel and went to bed. Surprisingly, she slept as soon as her head touched the pillow, not waking until dawn, when the roar of the traffic broke into her dreams.

It was strange to hear so much noise outside, after being used to the quiet of waking at Ben's home. The only noises there to disturb her slumber had been the calling of the birds and the faint creaking of the old trees near her window.

She lay in bed for a while, not particularly anxious to move. Her mind was filled with the dreams she had had in the night—all of Ben; they always were.

She closed her eyes and his image filled her sight—his hard-boned face, his rare golden eyes, flaring with light, his beautifully moulded mouth, gentle and relaxed, compressed with passion or anger. It was so vivid that she cried out softly and buried her face in the cool pillows.

Finally, of course, she had to get up, and take a shower. She piled her silvery hair into a neat bun at the nape of her neck and dressed in a cool white cotton trouser suit and flat sandals. She did not bother with any make-up, apart from a couple of coats of waterproof mascara to enhance her eyes, and left her room in search of some coffee.

She found James eating breakfast and talking on the telephone, in the lounge where they had taken tea the afternoon before. He waved her into the room and indicated the tray in front of him, still talking to the person on the line in cool, businesslike tones.

China poured herself some coffee and glanced idly around the room. It was cool and stylish, but a little too impersonal for her taste.

The floor was tiled in a deep terracotta colour, beautiful, but to her mind not very cosy, and the huge suite was of a square modern design in soft white leather. The walls were white, mostly bare apart from a couple of large paintings. Tall plants and a huge stone statue of a horse stood near the blind-covered windows. The whole room had a distinctly foreign air about it, she decided with a secret smile.

She finished her coffee and reached for a peach from the bowl on the table, slicing into its soft skin with a knife. James finished his telephone call and turned to her with a smile. 'Sleep well?' he enquired, pouring out more coffee for them both.

'Mm, surprisingly well. I went out like a light— probably all that ouzo.' She laughed, thinking how happy and relaxed James looked in an open-necked shirt and cotton trousers. She suddenly felt very glad to have him as a friend.

'What will you do today?' he asked, watching her as she delicately ate her peach.

'I don't know, I haven't really thought. Will you need any help here?' She was anxious to repay his kindness in asking her over for a holiday and offering her a job.

'You're supposed to be on holiday,' he reminded her laughingly.

'I know, but I could lend a hand if you're stuck.'

'Well, actually . . .' James looked rather sheepish, 'I have about thirty letters that need typing. I was going to ring an agency, but I've got interviews for an assistant chef at ten, and. . . .'

'Okay, okay, I get the message,' China cut in, unable to stop herself smiling at his deliberately helpless face. 'You're snowed under and I'd be very glad to help.'

'I was hoping you would be,' James admitted, unrepentant. 'I didn't like to ask, though.'

China pulled a face at him and lit a cigarette, rather glad that she had something to occupy her morning with. She had the feeling that time would weigh heavily on her hands if she was left to her own devices.

Ever thoughtful, James fixed up the typewriter and everything else she would need on a table on the balcony of the apartment, so that she could sit in the morning sun while she worked.

It was a nice idea, and it meant that she could watch the bustle below and feel the warmth of the sun on her face and arms.

The letters only took her a couple of hours, all being comparatively short, and breaking for coffee, she watched two dark-skinned young men refilling the hotel swimming pool below her.

They sang as they worked, and shouted to each other, waving their hands expressively. China watched them for quite a while, until one of them caught sight of her golden head and waved up at her, shouting something unintelligible in Greek. Blushing furiously, China tentatively waved back and decided that it was time to get on with her work.

Then it was lunchtime and James whisked her off to a business lunch with him, after which, she wandered around the shops in the city, looking at fashionable clothes and jewellery. She had no intention of buying anything, but it was good to look.

Gradually a week passed and she began to get used to Athens. Her life had a certain pattern to it that she clung to, needing some kind of prearranged order in everything she did. She filled every minute of her waking day, usually working with James in the mornings, then lunching with him, and if he did not need her in the afternoons, she would go sightseeing or lie on the pale beach getting a suntan, or wander round the shops, trying to familiarise herself with the city.

She thought she saw Ben in the street one afternoon. It was not him, of course, but with the bright afternoon light blinding her eyes, the resemblance seemed remarkable.

The man was standing on the pavement waiting to cross the busy road. He was wearing a dark suit and he was tall and muscular with gleaming dark hair.

China stopped dead in her tracks as she approached him, convinced that he was Ben. She could not breathe properly and she thought she would suffocate, her heart was beating so fast.

Then he turned towards her, perhaps sensing her panic-filled gaze, and she saw that it wasn't Ben. This man's face was ordinary, not even attractive, lacking the stark-boned beauty that made Ben's face unique.

Her breath was expelled noisily as she walked quickly away, unaware of the curious glances she was receiving. She found the incident very disturbing and could not manage to put it out of her mind for days afterwards.

News of Ben came one morning as she joined James for breakfast after yet another night of wistful dreams.

James stared at her strangely, as she poured out a cup of coffee for herself and sat down opposite him.

'You look very serious this morning. Not bad news, I hope,' she smiled.

Everything had been going so well with the hotel preparations that James had confided in her that he felt quite morose at times, half expecting disaster to strike at any second. It was all going *too* well, he had told her.

She had laughed at that and told him not to be silly, but all the same, his words had stuck in her mind and his confession had made her realise just how much the success of this venture meant to him.

Since then, she had been worried for him, nightly praying that everything would turn out right, constantly alert to his every mood. Thus, his frowning glance that morning immediately made her suspect the worst.

'No,' he replied, giving her a slight smile, 'not bad news. Ben rang this morning.' His voice was so ordinary, so casual, and it was such a bombshell that China choked on a mouthful of coffee, and the cup almost slid out of her hand, her fingers suddenly nerveless.

'From Egypt?' she managed, still coughing.

'No, he's back in England,' James said, quite calmly. 'He was worried to death, wondering where you were. I told him you were here—I hope you don't mind?'

'N-no, I don't mind,' she stammered, which was true, as she thought about it. So Ben knew where she was. It did not matter, she was hardly likely to see him again, and that was the important thing. Still, it was a shock, and it took her several traumatic moments to get over it.

James was still staring at her in that strange way. She took a deep breath, knowing now the reason for his odd mood.

'I'm sorry I didn't tell you the truth, but leaving Aspenmere Hall was very upsetting, I still can't talk about it without wanting to burst into tears,' she said very quietly, hoping that he would understand. He took her hand and squeezed it gently.

'I think I do understand. You love him.' China's head jerked up and he smiled. 'Yes, I knew the morning I called to see you. I also knew that I didn't have a chance with you,' he said ruefully. 'It was quite a shock, though, when he rang, sounding frantic and asking me if I knew where you'd gone.'

China was silent, shocked that her love for Ben was so obvious. She found it very difficult to believe that Ben had been worried about her. James was prone to exaggerate, as she knew from experience.

'How is he?' She had to ask, even though the conversation was very painful.

James' mouth twisted. 'The same as usual. He clinched the deal in Egypt earlier than expected, apparently, although he didn't sound particularly pleased about it. Ben's an enigma, as I'm sure you know.'

China nodded. 'Are you close to him?' she asked, suddenly thirsting for information. She had not talked about him for so long and now James had opened the floodgates on her curiosity again.

'We were close when we were kids, but Ben has always been a bit of a loner. He's very private, not easy to know—strong people rarely are. We drifted apart after we went to university and after he got his degree, he went off around the world and I didn't see him for three years. No, I don't think we are particularly close. Why?'

'You're very different, and I just wondered,' she said vaguely, secretly storing away all those scraps of information about Ben. They seemed very precious.

'I don't know whether to be flattered or not,' James said drily, then got to his feet, glancing at his watch and frowning. 'I'll have to fly, I have an appointment in ten minutes.'

'Is there anything you want me to do today!' asked China, as he grabbed his jacket and hunted for his car keys.

James paused and thought for a moment. 'Not that I can think of. Take the morning off—you deserve it. You can even pretend you're on holiday,' he teased.

Then he was gone and she was left to finish her breakfast in peace. She decided to stroll around the shops, an activity that she always found fascinating.

For some reason this morning, she felt very lonely. Maybe it was the talk of Ben that had brought on her melancholy mood.

She left the hotel half an hour later, after changing into jeans and a sleeveless blue tee-shirt. She slung her bag over her shoulder and walked to a part of the city that she had not yet explored.

She spent a pleasurable morning doing nothing in particular. The streets were hot, dusty and very busy, and she watched people going about their business and generally soaked up the atmosphere of the bustling foreign city.

By noon, she was hot and tired and her throat was parched. She found a pavement café with brightly covered tables, and sank down into a chair, thankful to take the weight off her aching feet.

She ordered a sandwich and an iced lemonade, her eyes faraway and dreamy. She did not see the tall figure approaching her table until he was standing right in front of her, staring down at her.

'Do you mind if I join you?' The low husky voice was unbearably familiar, her head jerked upwards and she found herself staring at the last person in the world she expected to see—Ben.

CHAPTER EIGHT

It was like a dream, and she felt as though she was about to faint. The whole world seemed to tilt, her half-eaten sandwich falling to the floor, and she clung to the edge of the table, her small knuckles white with strain.

Without waiting for her to answer, Ben pulled out a chair and sat down opposite to her, ordering coffee from a passing waiter. China stared at him with her heart pounding.

'You look as though you've seen a ghost,' he remarked sardonically, his golden eyes narrowed in scrutiny on her pale face.

'How . . . when did you get here?' she whispered, her wide eyes drinking in every inch of him. He looked tired, his dark face gaunt and closed, and there was a tenseness about his shoulders, suggesting that he had not slept for a long while.

'I flew in this morning,' he replied casually, as though it was the most natural thing in the world.

'Why?' she asked, suppressing her longing to fling her arms around him and tell him how she had missed him. Oh God, how I've missed him, she realised suddenly, even though he would never love her, even though he was having an affair with Olivia Daniels.

'To see James and to take a look over the hotel, protecting my interests, you might say.' There was a bitterness in his voice that she did not understand.

She had wanted him to say that he had come to see her, a crazy impossible dream, totally unthinkable, but somehow she felt unreasonably hurt by his words.

'What do you mean, your interests?' she asked curiously. 'The hotel belongs to James and Saul.' She could not keep the sharpness out of her voice. It was strange that they could be having this seemingly casual conversation after all that had happened between them, she found herself thinking, as she waited for his answer. It was as though they were merely polite acquaintances, although had their relationship ever really gone beyond that stage? she wondered miserably.

Ben frowned. 'Can I assume that James hasn't told you the full story, then?'

'Full story?' China echoed weakly, a sense of foreboding tightening her stomach.

'I lent him the money for the hotel. I own twenty five per cent of the shares,' Ben said flatly. It was quite a surprise and China did not know what to say. Why hadn't James told her? Ben was staring at her. 'You didn't know?'

She shook her head, still silent. There was a small pause, then he said, 'Why the hell did you run out on me?' There was anger in his voice and her startled eyes met his, surprised by his violence.

'I explained in the letter,' she said stiffly.

His mouth twisted with contempt. 'That pathetic scrap of paper told me precisely nothing.'

His words bit into her and she hit back like a frightened child, wanting to hurt him as he had hurt her.

'It should have been obvious,' she snapped.

'And what, in God's name, is that supposed to mean?' he demanded, totally ignoring the curious glances they were receiving from people at other tables.

'Don't try to intimidate me, it won't work,' China said coldly, and got to her feet. 'If you'll excuse me. . . .'

She surprised herself with her icy calmness as she walked away. She did not look back. Damn him to hell, she thought wildly, hardly able to see where she was going, her eyes were so fever-bright with tears. Why had he come here, shattering the fragile shell of her self-control, that had taken her weeks to build? She might have known that her flight from Aspenmere Hall had been too easy.

A low black car pulled up beside her as she stood on the edge of the pavement waiting to cross the road. Ben leaned over and pushed open the passenger door.

'Get in.' His tone was implacable.

'Go to hell,' she muttered, turning away.

'Get in, China,' Ben repeated. 'Now!' Something in his voice threatened her, telling her that if she did not do what she was told, it would be the worse for her.

So, obeying her frightened instincts, she slid in beside him, barely having time to shut the door before he shot away from the kerb, the wheels of the car squealing in protest.

She sat still and silent, as far away from him as possible, making her attitude obvious. Ben glanced at her once, his mouth a thin, hard line, but he said nothing. He drove into the suburbs, quickly and competently, handling the low, powerful car superbly in the heavy traffic.

The silence between them slowly built up into a nerve-stretching tension that made China want to scream. Finally the car slowed to a halt on a deserted stretch of road. She looked at Ben, apprehensively. He was staring straight ahead, the stark lines of his profile giving nothing away.

He lit two cigarettes and gave one to her. China found this small unimportant action overbearing. What made him think she wanted a cigarette? She was tempted to throw it out of the window, but common sense prevailed. It would give her something to do with her nervous hands, and to throw it away would be childish and rather silly.

'Nobody,' Ben said suddenly and tiredly, 'has ever made me as angry as you do, seemingly without even trying.'

'That's your problem,' China retorted quickly, not feeling at all sorry for him.

'On the contrary, it's your problem too,' he said grimly, flashing her a dark look from beneath hooded eyelids.

'Ben, why are we fighting?' China asked in a small voice. She felt very close to tears, raw, vulnerable and unable to bear his cruelty.

'Why did you run out, as soon as my back was turned?' he countered slowly, ignoring her pleading question.

China sighed, tempted to tell him the truth, but aware that she did not have the courage. 'I couldn't stay any longer, and James offered me....'

'Bloody James! It always comes back to him, doesn't it?' Ben cut in bitterly. He threw his cigarette out of the window in a strangely defeated gesture of violence and started up the car again.

Their conversation was obviously at an end and China sat back in her seat, feeling confused, but thankful that he had not made her give herself away and admit her love for him.

Ten minutes later, the car pulled up outside the hotel, and China jumped out and ran inside, not waiting to see if Ben said anything. She went straight to her room and collapsed on the bed, unable to control her shaking tears any longer.

She cried until she felt totally drained and empty, finally able to release the pent-up emotion that had been building up since she left England. There was a cold calmness inside her when she finally got up from the bed to wash her face, half an hour later, and she felt like a zombie. She examined her face in the bathroom mirror and almost smiled at the mess of her reflection, pale tear-stained face, red, swollen eyes, hardly an attractive sight. She splashed plenty of cold water around her eyes in an attempt to reduce the swelling, then brushed out her tousled hair and went to sit on the balcony of her apartment.

She lit a cigarette and stared at her hands, as she began to think. Ben owned one quarter of the hotel that she would be working in. It was shocking news, because she had thought herself free of him.

Her instinct was to leave, to hide from pain, but if she did go, she would be letting down James, who had come to rely on her help. He was expecting her to stay, and of course he knew nothing of what had happened between Ben and herself.

It was a difficult situation and one that she could not extricate herself from, without hurting James, who had been so very kind, and embarrassing herself. And if she was honest, she had to admit that there was nowhere for her to go, and why should she have to run from Ben? He did not know that she loved him, in fact he was under the mistaken impression that she was in love with James.

He would not stay in Athens for long; his business interests lay far and wide, and he was forced to travel a great deal. He also had a home in England, a home that she was sure he did not appreciate. Her thoughts were fierce as she remembered Aspenmere Hall with a deep rush of affection.

If she could treat Ben coolly and politely until he left, everything *should* be fine, and she had to admit that although seeing him hurt her, it also held a deep fascination. It was good to see him again, to be able to look at him, and hear him talk, even though it was hell, knowing that he would never care for her.

She would keep him at a distance, and when he left, her heart would probably break, but at least he would never know, at least she would have her pride, her job and the knowledge that she had not let James down. She stubbed out her cigarette, ignoring the small persistent voice inside her head that told her she would be left with nothing—nothing at all.

She heard the knock on her door, still deep in thought.

'Come in,' she called, not looking round, still working on her plan of campaign.

Seconds later, Ben appeared silently by her side. She looked up expecting it to be James, and her whole body stiffened, the smile dying on her lips as she looked into his devastatingly attractive face.

His gleaming dark hair was wet, and he had changed into tight, faded denim jeans that clung to his lean hips and strong thighs, and a sleeveless black vest that left bare his broad, smooth-skinned shoulders and powerful muscular arms.

'What do you want?' she asked, turning her eyes away and trying to keep her voice level. Her mouth was suddenly very dry, his nearness, his powerful sexual magnetism affecting her as strongly as always, making her wonder if she would ever be able to keep him at a distance.

'I thought you knew,' he replied softly, the insinuation obvious.

China flushed hotly, wishing that he would go away, but he moved to the edge of the balcony to stand in front of her, leaning back against the rail and crossing his arms across his broad chest.

His searching eyes moved slowly over her small face, taking in her paleness, her red eyes and vulnerable mouth, missing nothing, and she had to grit her teeth and force herself not to scramble to her feet and run to where he could not see her, to where those clever amber eyes would not be able to dissect her.

'I think it's time we talked,' he said slowly, still not taking his eyes off her.

'I don't know what we have to say to each other,' China replied lamely, unable to look into his face, her glance resting somewhere near his brown throat.

'Don't you? I'd have said there was a hell of a lot to talk about,' he said, sounding faintly irritated. His long body shifted restlessly. 'Dammit, China, look at us—we can't even manage a simple conversation!'

'That's because you have a vile temper,' she retorted, suspicious of his motives and afraid of her deep love for him. It would be far too easy and far too dangerous to make it easy for Ben.

'Yes, I have a vile temper, especially where you're concerned. I admit it, but you're hardly a paragon of patience yourself,' he said, his face hard, the muscle twitching in his jaw, evidence of the tension inside him.

China got shakily to her feet. 'I don't have to stay here while you insult me,' she muttered, still unable to look him in the eye.

He caught her arm, his fingers gentle but firm, and turned her inexorably to face him.

'I'm not insulting you, you crazy child.' His eyes were curiously tender. 'Come out for a drive with me—there's something I want to show you,' he added persuasively, his long fingers moving in slow, sweet caress on her bare arm, weakening her resistance to him.

She looked into his face, searching for signs of deceit, her heart suddenly pounding with slow languor as he smiled at her. All the warmth and charm in the world were in his smile at that moment.

'No tricks, I promise,' he said gently, as she hesitated.

'Okay,' she agreed, feeling reckless. It was an invitation too pleasurable to turn down. She seemed to have been alone for too long, starved of his company, and the price she would undoubtedly pay for this time with him suddenly seemed not to matter.

They walked out of the hotel and back to the car together, and Ben casually took her hand, his long brown fingers linking tightly with hers. China could feel the strength in that hand and her heart contracted. Anybody looking at us would think that we're lovers, she thought sadly, wishing with all her soul that it was true.

Neither spoke as they walked, but there seemed to be an easy companionship between them, for the first time, that precluded words.

They got into the car and less than half an hour later they reached a tiny harbour. It was bright and sunny and far too hot, the sun beating relentlessly down, making China feel weak, as they got out and she walked beside Ben, feeling his thumb moving rhythmically against the soft skin of her wrist.

'What's the matter?' He stared down at her, amber eyes fixed on the moisture beading her forehead.

'It's too hot,' she complained, with a small, child-like smile.

'Wait here.' He was gone before she could protest, so she leaned against the wall and looked out over the harbour, at the small, bright boats tied to the jetty, moving slightly on the sparkling water.

Ben was beside her again in minutes, holding a fine straw hat, with a long blue ribbon exactly the colour of her eyes, around the crown and a wide, shady brim.

He put it on for her, with gentle hands, pulling down the brim so that it shaded her eyes from the glare.

'Very fetching,' he said with a smile.

'Thank you.' She was touched by his kindness, her fingers straying over the finely-woven straw and the satin ribbon, ridiculously near to tears.

Without examining her motives or considering the possible consequences, China leaned up and kissed his mouth briefly, her lips moving innocently against the firm warmth of his.

She heard him draw breath, his long body tensing, his mouth not responding to her kiss, and realised her mistake, twirling away from him in misery.

'China. . . .' he began very softly, her name husky on his lips.

'What did you bring me here to show me?' she asked quickly, not wanting to know what he was about to say, feeling embarrassed and definitely unable to talk about what had just happened.

Ben paused, then took her hand again and led her along the wooden jetty to where a large yacht was moored, its smooth elegant lines taking her breath away.

'Yours?' she queried, already knowing the answer.

'Do you like her?' Ben's eyes were fixed on her rapt face.

'She's beautiful. I've always loved boats,' she laughed.

'Want to look round?'

She nodded and he helped her across the gangway on to the salt-stained wooden deck.

The yacht was called *Hallowe'en*, or so it said on the old shiny brass plaque on the wheel.

China walked right round the curved deck, trying to imagine what it would be like at sea. She had never been on a boat in her life before and she found that she liked it.

She opened the varnished door and went below, her fingers tracing the patterns on the lovingly-cared-for wood.

'Mind the steps, they're very steep.' Ben's warning voice was just behind her, making her jump, making it impossible for her to turn round and retrace her steps.

She went down carefully, as instructed, and found herself in a huge cabin, luxuriously furnished in a mellow, compact way.

She smiled, loving the huge round portholes and the clever way that everything in the cabin could be secured to the floor or the walls in stormy weather. The wood and brass gave everything a warm atmosphere.

She wandered into the galley and through into three other cabins all fitted with large beds, showers and toilets, every convenience. It was beautiful.

She strolled back into the main cabin and found Ben. He was looking at her, as she came in, watching her unselfconscious grace and the enthusiasm in her brilliant eyes.

'Would you like a drink?'

'Something cool, please,' she replied, watching him as he moved into the galley to open the small

refrigerator and pour her out some lime and lemonade.

He handed her the glass, his fingers brushing hers
for a second. China pulled away as though electro-
cuted, aware of his openly mocking glance.

'It's perfect,' she said lightly, needing to talk. 'I
didn't know you owned a yacht.'

'There's a lot you don't know about me.' Ben's
voice was wry, aware that she was desperately trying
to make conversation. 'I've had her for about a
year.'

'Have you sailed anywhere in her?'

'From St Lucia to here, that's all. She needed
some repairs and I haven't had very much free time,'
he told her with a casual shrug of his wide shoulders.

'If I had a yacht like this, I'd make time to sail in
her,' China said softly, her blue eyes alive with
dreams. 'I'd go round the world and never come
back.'

Ben laughed out loud, never taking his eyes off
her. 'Surely life here isn't so bad?' he taunted softly.

'I didn't mean. . . .'

'I know.' Their eyes met, locking fiercely, hers
wide and shadowed, his dark and inscrutable.
China's breath caught as pure electricity crackled
between them, their awareness of each other snaking
around them like bands of strong silk, filling the
cabin, filling her mind and all her senses.

Her fevered eyes dropped to the firm lines of his
mouth, and her own lips parted involuntarily. This
small movement caught Ben's eye and he reached
for her in one fierce, graceful movement, pulling her
against the hard, flat wall of his chest, one hand
tangling in her silky hair to pull back her head, exposing her innocent mouth and the long, slender line
of her throat to his glittering glance.

He lowered his head slowly and China, perfectly still, watched the hard bones of his face looming nearer, the sudden, intense flaring of light in his golden eyes, as he stared at her.

Then his mouth touched hers, burning like fire and ice, brushing over her parted lips, slowly, unhurriedly, teasing her, until with a small moan of pure need she lifted her slender arms around his brown neck and pulled down his dark head, admitting her hunger for him at last.

His kiss was deep and drugging, demanding the response that she eagerly gave, their mouths moving endlessly against each other.

His hand left her hair to travel downwards, stroking along her sensitive neck to her shoulders, to her breasts. Then he lifted her effortlessly into his arms, his mouth still urgent on hers, and carried her to the soft couch, moving somehow, so that she lay beneath him, trapped by his hands and the strong muscles of his thighs.

She felt the heavy weight of his body with pleasure, and her hands moved to his bare brown shoulders to caress him. Madness ran in her blood as she touched his warm skin, hearing him draw breath sharply, as his mouth left hers, sliding to her smooth, vulnerable throat, his hands moving beneath the loose waist of her tee-shirt, to find the soft skin of her stomach.

He was murmuring her name, his lips strangely cool against her heated skin, as he removed her top with sure, gentle hands. He looked down at her, breathing unevenly, his eyes dark with devouring desire.

'I've waited so long to hold you, to touch you again,' he said huskily.

China stared up into his hard face, her blue eyes

fevered, stunned by the raw need in his voice.

'Ben, my love, touch me,' she whispered.

He lowered his head immediately and she was lost, wanting only to please him, her heart beating desperately fast, its deep, sexual rhythm making her cling to Ben's muscular body.

His hands were moving on her, gently, exploringly, almost as if he was afraid to touch her. Her skin was warm and scented and felt like satin beneath his fingers.

His mouth moved across her throat then, to her slim shoulders, his tongue exploring the fragile hollows beneath her collarbone, then lower to her breasts, his hands sliding beneath her, palms flat against her spine, holding her trembling body still, as his mouth moved to capture and caress a taut nipple.

China moaned softly, her fingers clenching against his smooth shoulders, sensation filling her fierce sharp pleasure mingled with an aching need that only he could satisfy.

She opened her drowsy eyes and looked at his dark head bent to her white body, at his powerful brown arms coiled around her. He must never know how she loved him, how could he make love to her like this and not know?

Suddenly she was afraid, twisting in his arms. 'Ben, please. . . .' The fear was in her voice and he lifted his head immediately, easily reading her frightened face.

His eyes were dark and very tender and she could not bear such gentleness, such sweet concern. Her tears came quickly, rolling down her face as shame filled her. How could she let him touch her, kiss her like this when she knew that he did not love her? Was she mad? Yes, she was, mad with love for him.

Ben moved quickly and gracefully so that she lay beside him, wrapped in his arms, his mouth moving against her hair.

'China, I didn't mean to frighten you, I swear,' he said quietly, comforting her.

She lay perfectly still in his arms, aware of the tense, clenched muscles of his body as he fought to control his desire for her.

'I'm sorry,' she whispered, longing to touch him, caress him.

He smiled down at her with warm eyes, wiping away her tears. 'More apologies?' he teased, kissing her forehead.

Then he released her and got to his feet, agile and graceful, turning away from her, as he reached into his pocket for his cigarettes.

China silently thanked him for his tact as she pulled her tee-shirt back over her head and scrambled into a more dignified position on the couch.

Ben seemed completely in control of himself as he turned back, handing her a cigarette, his eyes blank and unreadable, the expression, or lack of it, that she was used to.

China felt dreadfully embarrassed.

'I ought to be getting back to the hotel,' she said with lowered eyes, just for something to say, to break the tense silence between them.

'Why?' Ben's voice was soft and warm, offering her heaven.

'James will be wondering. . . .' Her voice trailed off as his face froze. The mere mention of James was the red rag to the bull for Ben.

'And will you tell James what has happened between us this afternoon?' he queried harshly.

Hot colour stained China's cheeks. 'How dare you!' she whispered, shocked at his deliberate cruelty.

'I dare, China, because I want you, but you know that,' he said in a soft, dangerous voice. 'Perhaps I will tell James myself.'

'Y-you wouldn't. . . .' She faltered, staring at him in painful amazement. Surely he would not broadcast such beautiful intimacy as they had shared, with anyone caring to listen? As far as she was concerned, it was very, very private and she had no intention of telling James or anybody else.

'Oh, but I would. I'd do anything to get you in my bed. Does the thought displease you so much? Perhaps we can compare notes, James and myself,' he finished, with cold heartless cruelty, his mouth a hard, uncompromising line.

'You're a cruel, ruthless swine, Ben Galloway, and I hate you!' China declared vehemently, her body alive with pain.

Ben lifted his powerful shoulders uncaringly, his amber eyes totally blank. 'So you say. It was a different story five minutes ago, I could have had you so easily and you wouldn't have raised a finger in protest, so don't play games with me, China, we both know the truth.' There was a harsh, empty edge to his voice, that hurt her beyond words.

She got to her feet and ran from the cabin. Ben followed her, and in silence they drove back to the hotel. China felt numb and cold, unable to ignore the throbbing headache that was making her eyes ache badly. The moment they reached the hotel she jumped out of the car without a backward glance, and hurried inside.

James was in reception as she entered the building. He smiled at her brightly. 'Hi, been shopping? I like the hat.'

China snatched it off her head as though it was on fire, and scowled at him.

'Why didn't you tell me that Ben was coming here?' she demanded accusingly.

'Ben? Here?' James was obviously surprised. China nodded, still frowning. 'I've only just got back, I've been out all day,' James explained. 'Where is he?'

'I don't know,' she said, not quite truthfully, and hoping Ben had not followed her in. 'But I saw him this morning.'

'Are you sure it was him? He didn't say anything when he telephoned.'

'Of course I'm sure, I talked to him for ages!' China exploded, terribly exasperated.

'Okay—calm down, I'm sorry. I thought you might have just seen him from a distance,' James said placatingly.

China sighed. It was no good taking her bad temper and her headache out on James, it was not his fault.

'I'm sorry too. I've got a splitting headache,' she apologised. Then she remembered what Ben had said. 'Why didn't you tell me that he owns twenty-five per cent of the hotel?'

James flushed. 'Didn't I mention it?' He was being too vague.

'You know you didn't,' China replied.

'I didn't think it was important, I still don't. What difference does it make?' He was staring at her curiously as he asked.

'None, I suppose,' she admitted. He did not know about the bitterness between her and Ben, so he could not guess at the significance of not telling her. 'It would have been nice if you'd told me, though,' she added.

'I'm sorry, love, I really didn't think it was important. I didn't know you were interested in the business side of things.'

He looked quite shamefaced and she felt sorry for him.

'Oh, James, just ignore anything I say this afternoon, I'm not feeling too good. I think I'll go to my room, take a couple of aspirins and lie down for a while. I'll see you later.' She turned and made her way towards the lift, but he detained her.

'Oh, by the way, will you have dinner with me tonight? I've booked a table for eight. Please say yes, China.' He seemed hesitant about asking her, and openly enthusiastic, and she wished that she had not been so hard on him.

'I'd love to have dinner with you,' she said, smiling brilliantly, trying to make it up to him.

'Great! I'll see you in my apartment at seven-thirty, then. I hope the tablets work.'

She made her way up to her apartment and lay down in her cool, dark room, after taking the pain-killers. It had been a disastrous day.

So much for her ideas of keeping Ben at a distance; he only had to look at her and she melted inside. Stronger tactics were obviously needed. She fell asleep thinking of him.

It was late when she woke, just before seven, and she had to rush to get showered and ready for her dinner date with James. Her headache was a little better, but not gone completely, and she felt rather exhausted even though she had been sleeping all afternoon.

But the shower helped, the cool water dispelling the last of her drowsiness. She made her face up carefully, then dressed in a simply-cut pale yellow dress made of silk, that hinted at her slender curves and gave her hair the look of spun silver.

Creamy ivory earrings and silver bracelets, together with yellow high-heeled sandals completed her outfit. She had decided to leave her hair loose, but at the last minute coiled it on the top of her head in an elegant loop, leaving only fine tendrils free to caress her ears and the nape of her neck.

Much better, she thought, examining her reflection and deciding that she looked a good deal more sophisticated with her hair up.

It was well after seven-thirty, time to meet James. She quickly sprayed on some of her favourite perfume and grabbed her handbag and a gauzy yellow shawl, just in case the evening turned chilly, then left her bedroom, making her way to James' apartment.

She could hear James laughing as she approached the open door. Praying that he was not with Ben, she took a deep breath and entered the room.

Nothing prepared her for the shock that hit her, as James turned to greet her. For standing behind him was not only Ben, but next to him, looking very cool and very lovely as she stared up into his dark face, was Olivia Daniels.

CHAPTER NINE

IT was certainly a day for shocks, China thought with weary hysteria, hardly hearing James as he asked her what she would like to drink.

'I'm sorry?' She turned stunned blue eyes on him, aware that he had been speaking.

'Drink?' James repeated with a slight smile.

'A sherry would be fine,' China faltered, her eyes still glued to Olivia Daniels.

James followed her glance. 'Olivia and Ben will be joining us for dinner—you don't mind, do you?'

'Of course not,' she said weakly, suddenly aware of Ben's sardonic eyes on her face. What else could she say? She could hardly tell the truth.

It should have been obvious to her when she saw Ben this morning. She should have known that he would not come to Athens alone.

James handed her a glass. 'China, I believe you know Olivia.'

'Yes, we've met before.' China forced herself to smile at the other woman, who obviously did not intend to make the same effort.

Her cold opaque eyes flicked over China. 'You certainly get around, my dear,' she laughed delightfully. It was a veiled insult, cleverly disguised beneath that sweet laughter.

'So do you,' China replied with just as much sweetness. She was not in a servile position any longer and she did not have to be polite to Olivia Daniels. She would give as good as she got. 'Did you arrive today?'

'Yes, I begged a lift with Ben,' Olivia said languidly. 'Private planes are the only way to travel.'

China digested this information. She had known that Ben had his own plane, but it surprised her to learn that he had come to Athens in it. He must have been in a hurry.

Casting China a pointedly bored look, Olivia turned away and began chatting to James, making it obvious that she had nothing to say to the younger woman. China watched her. Olivia looked very beautiful tonight in a dark green chiffon evening gown with a tight bodice and dozens of tiny pleats falling from the waist. No wonder Ben wanted her! That thought hurt her and she turned away, to find Ben at her side.

'Bravo, my love,' he murmured softly, so that only she could hear. China glared at him, unable to stop her heartbeat racing away. He was wearing a black velvet jacket and black trousers. He looked dark and powerful and she could smell the faint scent of his cologne mingling with the clean male scent of his body. She felt the strong pull of his overpowering attraction and had to fight it.

'Where's Charles?' she asked coldly.

'In London, I imagine. He and Olivia are legally separated,' Ben replied flatly, as though these facts did not appeal to him. 'Olivia has come here to. . . .' He stopped abruptly, changing the subject. 'Can I get you another drink?'

He was urbane and charming, and China nodded, unable to speak as she handed him her glass. She did not really want another drink, but at least his absence would give her a few moments to pull herself together.

She knew that he had been about to say—Olivia Daniels had come here to be with him. It was shatteringly and heartbreakingly obvious, and it made the tense, passionate scene between her and Ben that afternoon seem very sordid. How could he have made love to her when he had only just arrived with Olivia? It was very strange.

Ben had shown himself to be honest, intelligent and gentle; honour and integrity were an inherent part of his character. So why did he behave this way? Perhaps he didn't like women, she thought hysterically, knowing that to be untrue. She had seen warmth and passion in him, in fact his sexual magnetism was one of the stronger facets of his complicated personality.

Perhaps one woman can't satisfy him, she thought next, feeling rather spiteful. But that did not ring true either, because for some strange reason, even though he was not married, she instinctively felt that he would be faithful when he loved.

She realised the truth of James' words. Ben was an enigma, and it had been proved beyond doubt tonight that Olivia was his lover.

She had been staring at him, she realised, and lowered her eyes as he returned to her side.

'You look very lovely tonight,' he said deeply, handing her another sherry. He paused for a second, then said, 'China, about this afternoon. . . .'

'Please, Ben, I don't want to talk about it, not now.' Her face was flaming as she cut across him quickly.

He stared at her for a moment, and she had the feeling that his fierce golden eyes could see right into her soul.

'Tomorrow, then,' he said implacably. 'We'll talk tomorrow.' She did not answer. She had no intention of talking about that incident, but it was useless to tell him so. She would have to keep out of his way for a few days, which would not be difficult, now that Olivia Daniels was here, she thought bitterly.

The restaurant was large and expensive and they were shown to a secluded central table, hovered over by deferential waiters.

China sipped a glass of wine, suddenly feeling rather ill and definitely not in the mood for eating out. Her appetite seemed to have disappeared completely.

She glanced around idly at the other diners, mostly wealthy Greeks, she guessed, and a party of Americans.

One of the American women was staring fixedly at Ben, obviously taken with his forceful good looks. She was being rather obvious, but glancing at Ben, China saw that he either had not noticed or was completely ignoring the woman.

He was talking to James about some confusing aspect of the hotel accounts. Olivia was sitting between them, her head turning prettily from one to the other, as she listened with apparently rapt attention.

For herself, China refused to be drawn into conversation despite efforts from Ben and James. She ordered a plain salad, ignoring Ben's eyes as they sharpened on her face.

'Won't you have something with it?' James asked, looking concerned.

'No, thanks. I find I don't feel very hungry,' she explained.

She watched Ben from beneath her lashes, awed by his smiling charm, listening to his clever, amusing conversation. She was feeling very strange, hot and cold with a sharp pain in her stomach and a throbbing ache behind her eyes. Her hands were clammy and her face was pale and beaded with cold perspiration. She pushed the salad restlessly around her plate, the mere sight of the gleaming black olives making her feel sick.

She would go to the ladies' room and wash her face. Perhaps that would help.

Excusing herself quietly, she got to her feet, alarmed at the way the room seemed to tilt.

She took a shaky step forward and for some reason her legs would not hold her, they seemed to be made of rubber. With a slight cry, she fell, nausea cramping her stomach. Oh God, I hope I'm not going to be sick in here, it would be too embarrassing, she thought numbly.

Ben was beside her in a second, so fast that she did not even see him move. He lifted her to her feet and she swayed against him, hardly able to stand without support.

Olivia was looking at her, a mixture of anger and distaste twisting her delicate features, obviously suspecting that the whole thing was some sort of attention-gaining trick, and James was looking worried, clearly at a loss to know what to do.

'I'll take you back to the hotel,' Ben said gently.

It was not what she wanted. 'But your meal. . . .' she stammered, clutching at her stomach as another wave of nausea hit her.

'To hell with the meal—can you walk?' His mouth was tight, his eyes shadowed with concern.

Olivia muttered something to James that China did not catch.

'I don't think so. . . . Oh, this is *so* embarrassing,' she moaned, aware of the interested eyes of other diners as they watched the little scene before them.

The head waiter came to the table, offering help, but Ben had already taken charge. He smiled, and touched her face. 'You can't help it,' he murmured,

and the next moment had swung her into his arms
as easily as if she was a weightless child.

'I'll take China back. Stay and enjoy your meal,'
he said to James, who was already getting to his feet.

'Yes, please do. . . .' China managed. It was bad
enough that Ben had to leave with her, she did not
want to spoil Olivia and James' evening. Ben walked
out of the restaurant with her in his arms. His
strength comforted her as she leaned against his hard
chest, her arms around his neck.

'I can get a taxi. . . .' she whispered, not wanting
to put him out.

'Don't be ridiculous,' Ben snapped, as they
reached the street.

She was violently sick as soon as they got outside.
Producing a handkerchief from his pocket, Ben
wiped her cold face with gentle fingers, then he
placed her in the car and drove back to the hotel.

He would not let her walk to her room, ignoring
her weak protests, as he lifted her into his strong
arms again and carried her upstairs.

Once there, he deposited her on the bed.

'Are you going to be sick again?' he asked quietly.

'I don't know,' she moaned, hardly able to bear
the sharp, tearing pain in her stomach. Ben stared at
her for a moment, then helping her to her feet, began
to undress her.

China wanted to protest, to tell him that she could
manage, but she knew that she couldn't, so she stood
perfectly still while he unfastened her yellow dress
and slid it off, her face red with embarrassment.

He removed all her clothes, quickly and gently,
his face totally blank, his eyes businesslike. Then he
slipped a thin cotton nightdress over her head and
ordered her to sit on the bed, whereupon he
unpinned her hair and brushed it out, braiding it

into one thick pigtail down her back.

China was overwhelmed by his concerned thoroughness as he helped her into bed and pulled the covers over her.

'I'm going to ring for a doctor. If you think you're going to be sick, call me.'

He left the room and she relaxed against the soft pillows. She had never felt so ill in her life.

The doctor who arrived half an hour later was small and round with a smiling, sallow face. He examined her quickly and efficiently and diagnosed mild food poisoning and heat exhaustion, telling Ben that she must stay in bed and not take any food. He left a prescription and then he was gone, and Ben with him.

China lay still in the large bed wondering how on earth she could have got food poisoning. Then she remembered the sandwich she had eaten at the outdoor café that morning. That must have been the cause.

Ben came back into the bedroom, moments later, smiling at her and carrying a bowl. He bathed her face with cool water and she stared up at him as he leaned over her, her feverish eyes riveted on his lean, beautiful face. He had discarded his velvet jacket and tie and opened his shirt low at the neck. China ached with love for him. He had been so kind tonight, so gentle and caring.

'Try and sleep now, child,' he said softly, drying her face and placing the bowl on the chest near her bed.

'Ben, will you stay with me for a while?' She felt very alone. There was something infinitely depressing about being ill in a foreign country. It made her feel insecure and frightened.

He stared down at her for a moment, his piercing

eyes easily reading her expression.

'Yes, if that's what you want,' he replied, pulling a chair to the side of the bed and sitting down.

Then China remembered his half-finished meal at the restaurant. 'Oh! Your dinner—you must go back—Olivia——'

'I'm staying here with you. Besides, I'm not hungry,' Ben said firmly. He got to his feet in a restless graceful movement, strolling over to the window and opening it, gazing over the city. China watched him.

There was a heavy weariness in the wide line of his shoulders, a stillness in him that made her think he was alone inside, and her heart cried out to him. She suddenly remembered what James had said. Ben was a strong man, difficult to know. She, for one, never knew what was going on in his shrewd, clever mind. Bad luck for me, she thought sadly.

The pain in her stomach had eased a little, and luckily, she did not feel as though she was going to be sick at any minute.

'How long will you stay in Athens?' she asked Ben, aware that she did not really want to know, it would hurt her when he did finally leave.

Ben shrugged, turning to face her, his amber eyes sardonic.

'Anxious to get rid of me?' he queried sardonically.

'No, I just wondered. . . .' Her voice trailed off lamely.

'I don't know. I have some business in the north, at Thessaloniki, so I'll be sorting that out before I leave. I'd like to be here when the hotel opens. And how about you, dear little China, how long will you stay in Athens?'

She did not answer immediately, digesting what

he had said. He would be here for quite a while, it seemed, and the news made her happy and sad at the same time.

'As long as James needs me,' she said finally.

Ben's face tightened, his jaw clenching with sudden anger.

'How very loyal,' he remarked savagely. 'I only hope James appreciates you.'

China frowned. 'I'm sure he does,' she said, her face puzzled, unsure of what he was getting at.

'And what payment are you exacting for this touching loyalty—marriage?' His eyes were contemptuous, his voice scathing.

She flushed. 'That's none of your business,' she snapped, hating him for his cruelty.

'James is my brother, I think that entitles me to make it my business,' Ben said coldly.

Sighing, China wished that she had never let him think that she was emotionally involved with James. The situation was getting out of hand.

'I don't think that James would thank you for your interference,' she said, matching his cold tone. 'Besides, I would have thought you had better things to concern yourself with.'

'Meaning?' Ben's voice was dangerous, and China closed her eyes to blot out the violence in his face.

'Meaning Olivia Daniels,' she said recklessly, opening her wide eyes again to stare at him in defiance.

The dark brows lifted in surprise. 'Do you think I'm having an affair with the lovely Mrs Daniels?' His voice was also surprised.

He's surprised that I know, China thought furiously.

'I don't give a damn.' Her voice was icy and she longed to slap the cold humourless smile from his mouth. Then a spasm of pain hit her and she gasped, scrambling out of bed and only just making it to the bathroom before she was sick.

Ben followed her, his eyes remote on her slender shaking body bent over the basin.

She felt humiliated. 'Why don't you leave me alone?' she whispered, as she splashed her face with cold water from the tap. She hardly wanted an audience when she was being sick.

'You asked me to stay,' Ben reminded her. 'And the doctor also suggested that I keep an eye on you.'

He helped her back into bed and sat by her, taking her cold hands in both of his, gently rubbing some warmth back into them.

China felt very tired, secure in his presence.

'I feel sleepy,' she muttered, her blue eyes moving on his face.

'Go to sleep, then,' Ben smiled as though she had said something funny.

She closed her eyes for a moment and before she realised it, had fallen asleep.

She woke once in the middle of the night, feeling sick. She fumbled for the light switch and snapped it on. Ben was asleep in the chair. She crept out of bed and wearily made her way to the bathroom. Then she went back to bed, half lying against the pillows as she watched him sleep. The harsh planes of his face were relaxed, the weariness gone, his mouth very gentle. She badly wanted to touch him.

At that moment his eyes snapped open and he stared back at her, instantly alert, his amber eyes becoming shuttered immediately.

'What's the matter?'

'I've just been sick again, if you must know,' China retorted petulantly, wishing that he hadn't spoiled her peaceful mood.

'Poor baby,' he taunted softly, raking his hand through the glinting vitality of his hair in a betraying gesture of weariness and strain. 'What time is it?'

She glanced at the clock on her bedside table. 'Four o'clock.'

'I'm going to get some coffee. Will you be all right?'

'I imagine so,' she said tartly, hungrily watching him as he got to his feet, stretching his powerful body indolently.

She switched off the light and thought about him while he was gone, a faint smile curving her soft mouth, and by the time he returned she was almost asleep, her blue eyes half closed, her body relaxed. He sat down by her and she could not read his expression in the dim light. She reached out her hand and he took hold of it, absently massaging the palm with his fingers.

She smiled sleepily at him. 'Will you kiss me, Ben?' she whispered, hardly aware that she was speaking aloud.

He moved, arching over her, his hands on either side of her reclining body, and kissed her mouth briefly and gently, his mouth warm and very sensual.

She smiled up at him brilliantly, hearing him draw breath.

'I wish I wasn't ill,' she murmured, longing for him to hold her, reckless in her sick, sleepy mood.

'So do I,' he muttered, kissing her face tenderly, his eyes glinting down at her in the darkness. 'Dear God, I want you—more than I've ever wanted anybody.' His voice was very low, intense, vibrant with his need for her, and all the time he was speaking, he was not touching her, merely arching over her, staring down at the white blur of her face, his breath cool as it fanned her cheeks.

She knew how he felt, because she wanted him—oh, how she wanted him! But she would never tell him, because to do so would reveal her love for him, and while Ben wanted her body, he did not want her love.

She heard him sigh heavily, then he moved away from her, sinking back into the easy chair by the bed.

'Do you mind if I smoke?' he asked abruptly, his voice harsh, rough.

'No,' China answered in a small voice. She turned on to her side, away from him, burying her head against the pillow, feeling inexplicably hurt and shaken.

The click of his lighter was the last sound she remembered before falling into a dreamless sleep.

When she woke, late the next morning, Ben was gone. She felt much better, no pain at all, but still a little weakness in her legs. She was very thirsty though, and swung herself out of bed, intending to get some water.

She walked slowly out of her apartment and along the plushly-carpeted main corridor in search of James, strolling into the lounge of his apartment. It was empty, but there was a jug of water on the low table.

As she reached for it, she heard laughter, unmistakably James', coming from the adjoining bedroom, and froze, rooted to the spot as she realised that he was not alone, her startled eyes suddenly alighting on a woman's dress slung carelessly on the floor behind the couch.

It was a green pleated dress—the dress that Olivia Daniels had been wearing for dinner the night before, and as if any further confirmation was needed, China suddenly heard Olivia's husky voice murmuring unmistakable words of love.

Her fingers tightened on the jug of water as the truth hit her like a ton of bricks. Olivia and James were lovers, she could hear them in the bedroom, and hot colour stained her cheeks as she left the room as quickly and as quietly as she could.

She ran straight into Ben in the corridor, and his arms reached out to steady her, his golden eyes flicking over her, taking in her tousled blonde hair, her slender body almost visible through the thin cotton of her nightdress, and bare brown feet.

'What the hell are you doing out of bed?' he demanded grimly, his eyes on the water jug that she was clutching tightly.

China stared at him in silence. He was only wearing brief shorts and a towel slung casually across his broad shoulders. His brown muscular body gleamed in the bright morning light, her mouth was dry and there was an aching lump in her throat. She was overpowered by his nearness, by the sheer force and potency of his attraction.

'W-water—I needed a drink,' she stammered, moistening her dry lips with the tip of her tongue in an unknowingly provocative gesture.

Ben took the jug from her nerveless fingers and sliding his hand beneath her elbow, propelled her back towards her room. Once there, he poured her a glass of water and opened the blinds, letting in the warm morning air.

'Now get back into bed and stay there,' he ordered, quite gently.

Casting him a dark glance that made him laugh, China did as she was told. She sat in bed, drinking her water with thirsty enthusiasm and glowering at him.

Ben watched her with unfathomable eyes, hands resting casually on his hips, a faint smile playing around the corners of his firm mouth.

'You're feeling better today, I assume?' he questioned drily.

'Yes, no pain at all, I just feel a bit weak,' she replied, pulling a face.

'Good. But I don't want to see you out of bed again. The doctor said you have to rest and that's what you're going to do. If you want anything—anything at all, shout and I'll hear you. Right?'

'You're such a bully,' China complained, pouring out another glass of water.

'With you I have to be,' said Ben, smiling at her.

He turned to go and she found that her eyes were fixed with painful intensity on the long brown sweep of his back.

'Ben, I want to thank you, for everything you did for me last night, bringing me back here and calling the doctor, and. . . .' she flushed, remembering how he had undressed her and put her to bed. 'I appreciate it, and I didn't mean to spoil your evening,' she added hurriedly, wanting to detain him for some reason she did not care to examine too closely.

Ben turned at the door, flashing her a defastating smile. 'You don't need to thank me, and you didn't spoil my evening. You're very beautiful when you're asleep,' he said softly, and left the room.

China lay back against the pillows, a tiny shiver of excitement running through her at his words. Had he watched her sleeping? Goodness, I hope I don't snore or sleep with my mouth open, she thought in horror.

Her mind turned to Olivia and James. She was appalled by Olivia's duplicity. She had come here with Ben, was obviously his lover, and now she was sleeping with James. It was shocking and rather heartbreaking.

Did Ben know? How could she? China thought sadly, praying that Ben wouldn't be hurt. If Ben were my lover, I wouldn't even be able to look at another man. I can't anyway, and there's nothing between us, except my love and the occasional spark of mutual desire.

James came in to see her later in the morning. He looked very happy, and China felt uncomfortable in her knowledge of Olivia and him.

'How are you feeling?' he asked cheerfully, perching himself on the side of the bed and running a casual finger down her cheek.

'Much better, and I'm sorry about last night.'

'No problem,' James shrugged. 'As long as you're feeling better.'

'I am. Where's Olivia?' She could have bitten out her tongue. The careless question had just slipped out, she hadn't been thinking straight.

James cast her a sharp look. 'She's gone shopping, I think. Why?' He was rather suspicious. It was no good, she had to tell him, she was no good at pretence, and sooner or later she would probably say something, unthinkingly, that might embarrass him.

She took a deep breath. 'James, I don't know how to say this, but . . . well, I heard you and Olivia this morning. . . . I . . . I was looking for some water and . . . oh, I'm making such a mess of this, I shouldn't have said anything!' She felt tactless and utterly miserable.

James flushed, his fingers fiddling with the covers on the bed. 'As you know I might as well tell you the rest of it. I'm in love with Olivia, and as soon as she gets her divorce, I'm going to marry her.'

China was stunned. '*She's* the woman you told me

about?' she asked faintly.

James nodded. 'I couldn't tell you at the time because she was still with Charles, but now they're separated, I don't suppose it matters. I know you and Olivia haven't exactly hit it off, but she's really quite shy, do you know? If you got to know her, really got to know her, as I do, I'm sure you would both be firm friends.' He was asking for her approval and China smiled at him gently.

'I'm sure we would be,' she lied, knowing that she would never be able to get on with Olivia. 'Does Ben know?'

'No. Olivia wants us to keep it quiet until we announce the engagement,' James said, sounding quite wistful, as though he wanted to shout it from the rooftops.

I'll bet she does, China thought to herself. Ben would not be pleased to find that Olivia was seeing James.

'I shouldn't have told you really, but you are one of my best friends. Will you promise not to tell anyone, not even Ben?' James begged.

'Yes, I promise,' China reassured him, running shaking fingers through her hair, feeling confused and very sad for Ben.

'You're very quiet, love. Aren't you pleased for me? I've never been in love before, it's wonderful!' His face was wreathed in smiles as he took both of her hands.

China managed a smile. 'I'm very pleased for you, silly, and I wish you all the luck in the world.' She tried to sound bright. 'You'll have to excuse me, but I still feel a bit weak, and this news has come as quite a surprise.'

She squeezed his hands, wishing that she could warn him about Olivia. She couldn't, of course, he would not believe her anyway; his love was certainly blind.

'How are things with you and Ben?' James asked, suddenly sympathetic.

'The same as usual,' China replied with a sigh.

'He was very protective last night,' he said speculatively. 'A good sign, don't you think?'

'Not really. I know you're trying to cheer me up, but I know that he'll never love me,' China said sadly, not wanting to talk about it.

'I'm sorry, I didn't mean to upset you.' He was embarrassed.

'You haven't,' she smiled, convincingly.

'I'll let you rest, then—doctor's orders, according to my dear brother,' James said cheerfully, jumping to his feet. 'Can I get anything for you?'

'No, thanks.' Hot tears were rising in her throat as he turned to leave the room. She wanted to shout after him, warning him. Charles, Ben and now James. Olivia destroyed people so easily. She said nothing, though, but let him go. then buried her head in the pillow, letting her tears fall unchecked.

Over the next few days, China spent most of her time in her room.

Ben had driven up the coast and would be away for at least three days, and James was wandering around in a happy daze, visiting her regularly and working hard.

Olivia came to visit her once, carrying a large bunch of flowers and a false smile. It was a short visit, the conversation stilted and unnatural. Not for the world could China pretend that she liked the older woman, and she was thankful when she left.

She felt quite well enough to get up now, but she did not bother, pretending to James that she still felt weak. She had all her meals in her room and she felt wrapped in a fierce melancholy, listless and uncaring about the time she spent just lying in bed, staring at the ceiling.

It was good for James, she supposed, her being out of the way all the time, because it meant that he could devote all his attention to the woman he loved. China felt very worried about him, instinctively knowing that Olivia would hurt him, sooner or later. James deserved better.

She wrote to Clare and Paul, telling them how she found herself in Athens. They would be back from their honeymoon in Mexico, and she did not want to lose touch with Clare.

She thought about Ben a lot too, her love for him so powerful that it was like a pain inside her. She always turned to him for comfort and he always gave it, generously, tenderly, without even thinking.

If he loved Olivia, then he would be hurt when he found out that she was going to marry his brother. She felt sure that he would not come to her for comfort. He would tear himself to pieces inside, alone.

I wish I'd never got involved with this family, she thought desperately, aware, even as the thought formed, that she was lying to herself. She would love Ben for as long as she lived, even though her life would not be worth much without him. At least she had loved, and that did not happen to everybody.

An important experience, she thought gloomily, wishing that she had let Ben become her lover. At least she would have had the memories of a night spent in his arms, to dream about for the rest of her life.

She also felt depressed because her future was once again very vague. Once James married Olivia, she expected that she would have to leave the hotel, always assuming that she took the job James had offered. Whatever she decided, ultimately, she would have to leave, and the question was, where would she go? What would she do? Would there never be anybody to offer her love and security? she wondered to herself.

She rescued her Italian painting from her suitcase, one afternoon when she was feeling particularly miserable. She had intended to leave it with the rest of her possessions at Mrs Stephenson's house, but at the last minute had removed it from the packing case and put it at the bottom of her case.

She stared at it for hours that afternoon, and when Ben found her she was lying on the bed, dressed in a violet-coloured sundress, with her arms wrapped protectively around the painting, staring up at the ceiling with a concentrated frown, as she wondered about the mess she was in.

He entered the room silently, watching her for long moments before he spoke.

'James tells me that you haven't set foot outside this door since before I left for Thessaloniki. What are you playing at, China?'

She jumped, startled to hear his voice but not daring to look at him.

'I haven't been well,' she said defensively, tightening her hold on the painting.

'Don't talk such bloody rubbish,' Ben said harshly, walking over to the bed with an easy animal grace that made her catch her breath. 'You were well enough the day I left, so what the hell's going on?'

She felt the mattress shift beneath his weight as he sat down on the bed beside her. She turned to face him, at last, her heart stopping for a moment as she looked into his beautiful, hard-boned face.

'Why should you care? Why don't you leave me

alone?' she demanded petulantly, her need for him making her aggressive.

'I wish I could,' Ben muttered, half to himself. He stared down at her. 'What is it, child, can't you trust me?' His voice was suddenly low and gentle, and she felt near to tears, bruised by his concern.

'There's nothing wrong,' she said stiffly. 'I haven't felt like going out, that's all.'

'Will you come out for dinner tonight?' Ben asked quietly.

'Why don't you ask Olivia?' she flashed at him.

'I'm asking you,' he replied. implacably.

'Yes,' she agreed tonelessly.

She could tell him nothing, so she had to agree to his plans, otherwise she knew that he would not give up.

He smiled and reached for her, pulling her off the bed and on to her feet. He stared down at her, his amber eyes searching, on her small pale face.

'What's that?' He indicated the painting she was still clutching in her arms.

'My favourite picture in the whole world,' she admitted shyly, showing it to him. 'Do you like it?' It seemed incredibly important that he did.

He looked at it in silence, for what seemed like ages.

'Yes, I like it. It's beautiful, and very good. I remember it on your wall at home.'

The way he said 'home', so casually, touched something raw inside China. *His* home, not hers, not now, not ever. Tears filled her eyes and she lowered her head.

Ben caught her abrupt movement and tilted up her chin with strong sensitive fingers, frowning heavily as he saw her tears. 'China, my love, you're so unhappy,' he murmured, his voice groaning.

'Can't you tell me about it? Is it James?'

She shook her head silently, and he bent down and kissed her mouth briefly, with warm hard lips.

Then he released her, reaching into the pocket of his jeans and drawing out a long flat package.

'This is for you,' he said, changing the subject, aware that she could not be pushed into disclosing the reason for her misery. He put it into her hands and she stared at him with wide, tear-washed eyes. 'Open it.' She tore off the paper and opened the box inside. It was a bracelet of silver, set with vivid blue stones, the exact colour of her eyes.

'It's lovely!' she breathed. 'But why?'

'To go with the hat,' he replied flippantly. 'I'll see you at seven-thirty.'

Then he was gone, not giving her a chance to thank him for the bracelet.

She smiled to herself, surprised to find that she was actually happy for the first time in days, finally admitting to herself that she had missed Ben dreadfully.

Olivia and James did not join them for dinner. Olivia was visiting friends and James had a business meeting. China and Ben dined with one of Ben's American business associates, and his wife.

It was a lighthearted evening, and China enjoyed herself immensely.

Ben watched her all evening with a strange, hungry intensity, smiling tenderly when he caught her admiring the silver bracelet on her slender wrist.

He kissed her lightly on the mouth, holding himself back, when they returned to the hotel, and she climbed into bed feeling tired but happy. Oh, Ben, I'm so very glad that you're back, she thought, before she fell asleep.

CHAPTER TEN

CHINA lay in the bath, languidly soaping her body as she wondered what she would wear. The water was warm and scented with her favourite bath crystals, and she relaxed with a happy sigh. A bath seemed to be an unaccustomed luxury these days, a quick shower being all she usually had time for.

Tonight she would attend the party for the opening of the hotel, a very big occasion, and she wanted to look her best. She shampooed her hair vigorously, then deciding to set it, so that it would curl around her small face. As she stepped out of the bath, she glanced at her watch on the shelf. She had just over three-quarters of an hour to get ready.

It had been, to say the least, a very hectic day, helping James with the preparations, organising the flowers, checking on the caterers and getting round to the thousand and one other things that had to be done.

Saul, James' partner, had arrived from the States at lunchtime. He was short and dark and very quiet. His shrewd eyes had been admiring as James had introduced China, and she liked him.

Saul had stayed in the hotel for exactly half an hour, then had hurried out for a meeting with the bankers, and she had not seen him since.

She had been worried at the strain clearly visible in James as the day wore on. He was nervous and irritable, snapping at people around him, including China.

There had been no sign of Olivia, or of Ben, who

had been working on a property deal on the other side of the city.

Her relationship with Ben had eased over the past two or three days. They did not argue any more. He was always polite, yet withdrawn and remote, and they were getting on well together in a superficial kind of way.

Dressed in a thin cotton wrap in a brown floral design, China set and dried her hair, then opened her wardrobe and flicked through her clothes with dissatisfaction. She wanted to wear something beautiful and stunning, but none of her dresses seemed to fit the bill. Olivia would look gorgeous, of course, and China could not hope to compete with her, but she wanted to try.

Then suddenly she remembered a dress that Clare had lent her, ages ago. It was in her suitcase, brought to Athens by accident, with the rest of her clothes.

She pulled out her suitcase from on top of the wardrobe and snapped it open, rummaging through the layers of tissue paper with excited hands, until she found the dress.

It was perfect, a tight seductive sheath of deep, metallic blue material that caught the light as the wearer moved, cut in a simple, daring style with a low, strapless, sleeveless bodice. Perfect.

She held it up against her body and looked in the mirror. She would not have dreamed of buying this dress for herself, it was far too sensual, too revealing, but for tonight, it was exactly right.

She made up her face very carefully. Her complexion was flawless and lightly tanned, needing no artifice, so she concentrated on her eyes, using kohl and pale, shiny shadow, and lastly, mascara, with a skill learned from Clare one rainy afternoon soon after China had returned from Italy.

The result was stunning, her eyes two huge pools of misty blue magic in her pointed face. She lightly brushed highlighter over her cheekbones, then painted some colourless lip gloss on to her mouth, and her face was finished. She examined herself carefully in the mirror, pleased with the results of her work. She looked quite beautiful.

She unpinned her hair and brushed it out until it fell in bright shining waves around her slim tanned shoulders, and dabbed her pulse spots with a light, haunting perfume, before slipping the blue dress over her head, struggling to zip it up.

When she looked in the mirror again, she was amazed at the transformation. The dress moulded her slender figure perfectly, leaving bare her golden shoulders, its deep colour working some magic on her eyes.

She hardly recognised the alluringly lovely young woman who stared back at her from the glass. She slipped on Ben's bracelet, deciding not to wear any other jewellery, the dress was enough, and stepped into high-heeled sandals.

She was ready ten minutes early, and if she went down now, James would probably bite her head off, so bad-tempered was he today.

So she strolled out on to her balcony, breathing in the warm balmy air of an Athens evening. The balcony was strewn with clay pots of flowers, their exotic scent mingling with the faint warm smell of the busy traffic below. It was a beautiful clear evening, the sky soft clear velvet as the moon rose. She was beginning to fall in love with this city, not a wise thing to do in the circumstances.

A faint noise turned her head and two balconies along from her own she saw, with a leaping heart, Ben, lighting a cigarette. He was sitting in a low chair, his feet up on the railing, staring into the night as he idly smoked.

He had not seen her, and she drew back a little into the shadows, to watch him. Once again she noted a strange loneliness about him, a tension in the powerful lines of his shoulders. She stared at his stark remote profile, aching with love for him, longing to go to him and ease whatever troubled him. I could make him forget, she thought with fierce sadness; I love him so much that I could make him forget everything.

A tap on her door broke her out of her reverie and she went inside, glad that Ben had not seen her. James was at the door and he whistled long and appreciatively as he saw her.

'You look incredible!' he said with a wide smile. 'Absolutely incredible!'

'Thank you.' China smiled back at him, pleased and amused at his extravagant compliments.

'I want to apologise for giving you such a hard time today,' he added. 'I have no excuse—I'm sorry.' He was like a little boy and China laughed and kissed his cheek, forgiving him immediately.

They went downstairs together to find that the guests had already begun arriving and she was soon separated from James, as he hurried about, seemingly tireless, bursting with energy, as he greeted people and chatted.

Ben appeared at her side five minutes later, his eyes narrowing as they slid over her seductive body, coming back to rest on her flushed and lovely face.

'You look beautiful,' he said slowly, in a low, husky voice. China sipped her wine and smiled at him, noticing the sudden flare of light in his amber eyes as she did so.

'Do you like my dress? I borrowed it from Clare,'

she admitted honestly, twirling her glass in suddenly nervous fingers.

'It's breathtaking,' Ben replied, his hooded eyes skimming over her slim bare shoulders. There was a roughness in his voice that jerked up her head, and she stared up into his face curiously, unable to read his expression.

He looked heart-stoppingly attractive tonight in a white dinner jacket, expensively tailored to his powerful body, and black slim-fitting trousers. Just looking at him sent weakness flooding through her body. Why couldn't he love her?

She glanced around the room, her eyes finding James and also finding Olivia, who had just arrived. She looked beautiful in white silk and lace, and China suddenly felt rather obvious in her bright dress.

'She looks gorgeous,' she murmured, half to herself.

'Who?' Ben had caught her words and was intrigued.

'Olivia,' she answered tonelessly, feeling unaccountably depressed and unable to hide it.

'Yes.' Ben's one word answer was flat and noncommittal. Did he know about Olivia and James? Did that explain the fierce tension in him?

China sighed, sick and tired of all the undercurrents, all the deceit. Everything was so complicated, everything except her love for Ben, which was pure and simple and driving her insane. She excused herself and escaped to the ladies' room.

When she returned to the party, Ben was dancing with Olivia, who was clinging to him unashamedly. China's eyes fixed on them painfully as she began to mingle. Damn him!

She forced a brightness she did not feel as she chatted to people, dancing with James and Saul, laughing a lot. The wine she was drinking was help-ing as well.

The party was a great success, and after an hour or so China had almost managed to throw herself into the mood of it, sparkling with a brilliance that drew people to her, especially men, aware of Ben's blank golden eyes upon her from time to time.

She felt reckless, uncaring as she deliberately ignored him, keeping as far away as possible.

She had just emerged from the ladies' room, late in the evening, when she was accosted by an American friend of James', who was clearly very drunk indeed. He lurched towards her, his un-attractive face red, his eyes hot, as he blocked her way in the narrow corridor.

Imagining that he would be fairly easy to handle, China flashed him a cool, wary smile. 'Excuse me, Mr . . .' she began pointedly.

'Call me Andy, honey.' His voice was slurred, and he made no effort to get out of her way.

'Will you let me past, please, Andy,' China said very coolly, feeling the first faint stirrings of alarm in her stomach.

They were quite a way from the party and nobody would hear her if she called for help, not through all the noise of music and chatter. He must have followed her, and the thought was frightening.

'No chance, baby. I've been watching you all evening.' His small hot eyes veered insolently over her body. 'And I like what I see. How about it—you and me—we could have a good time?'

He leaned towards her and she felt sickened by the raw spirit she could smell on his breath.

'Let me go,' she said icily, trying to get away from him. But somehow he had managed to back her into a corner and she could not move.

The man laughed, loud, ugly laughter that made her blood run cold.

'Very clever, but it won't work, not in that dress— you've been asking for it all evening.' He lunged towards her and China aimed a kick at his shins, frozen with panic now, memories of Signor Cencelli crowding into her mind, frightening and disgusting her.

The man swore obscenely as her shoe hit home.

'If you don't let me go, I'll scream the place down,' she threatened through teeth chattering with shock.

'Try it,' the man invited unpleasantly, his hot hand grabbing her bare shoulder in a rough caress that sent a shiver of pure cold revulsion down her spine.

Blind and shaking with fear, China screamed as loudly and as piercingly as she could, and in the next second, as if in a dream, she saw Ben's cold furious face, his golden eyes narrow intimidating slits, his powerful body threatening violence as he spun the other man round to face him, his fist crashing against the drunk's jaw with a sickening thud.

China turned on her heel and ran, driven by fear and sick of the violence and ugliness, ignoring Ben as he called to her.

She rushed out of the hotel on to the warm dark street, needing to get away from everyone for a while, including Ben. Where would she go? She remembered his yacht. She could get a taxi, and nobody would think of looking for her there.

There was a taxi rank outside the hotel, and China scrambled hastily into the nearest one. Luckily she had remembered the name of the tiny seaside town where Ben kept his yacht, and in less than half an hour they had arrived there.

She found Ben's yacht quickly, scrambling across

the gangway and collapsing on the deck, the heel
snapping off one of her sandals as she sank to her
knees.

Her face was wet with tears that she had not even
noticed, and getting to her feet with difficulty, she
crept below into the main cabin.

It was shadowy but not completely dark, the lights
of the harbour and the surrounding boats twinkling
through the round portholes. There was noise and
music coming from a small boat nearby, a party.

China found some cigarettes on the table and lit
one, drawing the smoke deep into her lungs in an
effort to calm herself, and curled up on a softly up-
holstered chair, staring into the darkness with wide,
unseeing eyes.

She guessed she had overreacted at the party, but
that whole scene had been so ugly and so frightening,
and so much like Italy, that she had lost her head
and run away.

It was good to be here, though, she felt safe and
unthreatened and alone on the yacht.

An hour later she was fairly calm, but totally
unprepared, as the door of the cabin was flung open
and Ben faced her.

He switched on one of the small wall lamps, bathing the cabin in a warm glow of light, and stared
at her without speaking, taking in her tousled hair
and pale, tear-stained face as she gracefully huddled
in her chair.

'I thought you might be here,' he said softly,
walking into the cabin and shutting the door.

She stared up at him with wide, blank eyes. He
could obviously read her very well.

'Won't you be missed at the party?' she asked
dully.

Ben shrugged, lighting a cigarette with indolent

ease. 'I doubt it,' he said with a faint smile. He seated himself on the edge of the table, very near to her, and unaccountably, she suddenly felt very shy, not knowing what to say.

'How are you?' he asked, reaching out and tilting her face towards him.

'Okay,' she whispered, feeling the touch of his fingers like fire on her cold skin.

'Did he hurt you?' His voice was harsh.

China shivered, shaking her head. 'Did you hurt him?'

'Not as much as I would have liked to. He was out cold after one punch.' There was a rough satisfaction in his face and his voice.

China moved restlessly in his grasp and he dropped his fingers from her face.

He was staring at her, his clever eyes probing, assessing her reactions, and she flushed, turning her head away from him, desperately aware of him, his nearness, the attraction that she could not resist.

'I'm leaving Athens,' she said suddenly, telling him her decision because she wanted something to say. The silence between them was stretching her nerves beyond endurance.

'Where will you go?' She sensed the stillness in him without turning to face him.

'It doesn't matter—anywhere,' she replied dully, feeling perilously near to tears.

'You could come back to Aspenmere Hall with me,' Ben suggested quietly.

'No, I couldn't,' she replied in a small voice, touched by his kindness.

'Why not? It's a job, and you'll need a job,' he said harshly.

She turned on him, instantly angry, shouting. 'Yes, I'll need a job, but I need more than that, I need something permanent, some security!'

Her voice was shaking, her wide eyes flooded with tears. I need love, she was silently screaming at him, your love.

'Won't James offer you that permanence, that security?' Ben questioned, his mouth twisting. 'He has Olivia, he doesn't need me,' she said coldly. She had not wanted to be the one to tell him about Olivia and James, but he would have found out in the end, and at that moment she did not care. She looked at him. The news had hardly shattered him, his face was as remote and as enigmatic as ever.

'Does that hurt you?' he probed gently.

'I want him to be happy,' she replied stiffly, aware that she was treading on very shaky ground.

Ben swore beneath his breath and got to his feet with angry grace, pacing across the room.

'I can offer you permanence and security. You can marry me,' he said in an expressionless voice.

China stared at him, her eyes dark with pain, hating him for offering her his pity.

'If this is your idea of a joke. . . .' she began furiously, but he cut across her.

'I don't find it remotely funny. It's a serious offer—the security you want and I can give.'

She wanted to hit him.

'At what price?' she enquired, icy with sarcasm.

Ben sighed heavily, his amber eyes totally unfathomable as they raked over her.

'No price. I won't even touch you unless you want it,' he said flatly.

'No!' she muttered forcefully, getting to her feet and walking towards the cabin door. She could not marry him. It would be agony to be married to a man she loved with all her soul, knowing that he did not care for her, that all he offered was pity. Ben was just being kind and she could not bear it, or perhaps his offer was aimed at getting back at Olivia. Whatever his reason, she wanted nothing to do with it.

She did not reach the door. In one lithe movement Ben blocked her exit, his hands reaching for her bare shoulders in a cruel, angry grip.

'Why the hell not?' he demanded, his eyes dark and violent. 'Is it still James?'

'No, no!' she shouted, twisting futilely in his grasp. 'It's never been James, I've never cared for him in that way.' The truth was out at last and she did not care, in fact she felt as though a heavy weight had been lifted from her heart.

'You let me believe you loved him—why, for God's sake?' Ben's voice was quieter, but it still held anger.

She did not answer, could not tell him of her love.

He shook her slightly, almost beyond control, watching as her pale hair tumbled around her tear-stained face.

'Tell me, China. Goddammit, let's have some truth between us, for once!' he grated.

China felt limp and hurt beneath his biting fingers. She stared into his lean furious face. If he wanted the truth, he could have it, she was suddenly past caring.

'You were having an affair with Olivia Daniels,' she said, her voice clear with defiance, satisfied at the shock she saw in his eyes.

'No,' he replied flatly, as though the very idea repulsed him. 'Not now, not ever, and there's been no one since I met you. How could there have been?' he asked simply.

'I . . . I don't understand,' she faltered, utterly confused, a tiny seed of hope bursting inside her, heating her whole body as she stared at him, her lovely eyes wide with innocence.

'Don't you?' Ben's eyes were suddenly filled with light and his long fingers became gentle against her skin. 'Don't you understand that I've loved you for what seems like all my life, that I'll always love you?'

China drew a long, shaking breath, hope shining in her brilliant eyes, unable to speak. Ben sighed again. 'And all the time I've loved you, James has been between us, and if you don't love him. . . .' He broke off, searching her face with fierce hungry eyes.

'Ben, I love you,' China whispered, reaching up to touch the hard bones of his face, wanting to end the torment she saw in his eyes.

He drew breath sharply and unevenly, pulling her into his arms, his mouth finding hers with hungry precision, groaning at her unashamed response. China wound her slim arms around his neck, stroking his hair and pulling him closer, moulding her body to the hard warmth of his. Finally he lifted his head, his eyes glittering with desire and love as he stared down at her.

'Marry me, China,' he begged in a low voice. 'My life is pale and empty without you, just a useless, endless drive for wealth and power.'

She lay in his arms, her mouth bruised by his urgent kiss, her long shining hair against his shoulders, her love for him burning in her blue eyes.

'Yes, I'll marry you, Ben, my love,' she said softly, feeling his arms tightening involuntarily around her as she spoke. 'But Olivia. . . . I saw her coming from your room, the day you left for Egypt. . . .' she whispered in a small voice.

Ben kissed her mouth gently. 'But what you don't know is that she came there uninvited, and I promptly threw her out. I swear to you, China, there's never been anything between us—she's a bitch, a cold spiteful bitch. She chased me, sure, but I turned her down flat. I loathed her for what she'd done to Charles. Now she's got her claws into James—I didn't think you knew, I was hoping to protect you from it.' He was telling the truth, and China cursed herself for deliberately thinking so badly of him.

'I saw them together one morning and James told me that he was in love with her. I thought you'd be hurt, that you loved her,' she said painfully.

Ben smiled down at her, his beautiful mouth frankly sensual. 'You crazy child, I don't give a damn for her, and I can even feel quite sorry for James, now I know you don't love him.'

China laughed. 'You were very mean to me,' she said accusingly, teasing him gently.

'Yes, I know—forgive me, my love. When I found you in my shower, calling for James, after you'd been in my mind every single day since I nearly knocked you down, I thought you belonged to him, and it was like a kick in the guts. I was cruel because I loved you, even then, and the thought of you with him made me want to kill you—and him. Every time I held you, felt your response, I was thinking that you loved him. I was crazy with wanting you, my only hope was that you always came to me for comfort. I hadn't slept for three nights before I went to Egypt, and I only went because I didn't think I could keep my hands off you. I was so crazy with worry when I got back and you were gone, I phoned James and flew out immediately.'

'With Olivia,' China said, mock-angry.

'She was at the airport waiting to fly out here to see James. She asked if she could come with me, and

I didn't care, I just wanted to get to you,' he explained. 'I treated you badly, I know, but I'll make it up to you, every day of our lives, I promise.' His mouth was warm and disrupting against the sensitive skin of her throat.

China touched his hair with wondering fingers, stroking its gleaming thickness. She felt so happy, she thought she might die.

She told Ben and he laughed. 'When will you marry me?' he demanded, staring at her with his heart in his flaring golden eyes. 'You need someone to care for you—and I promise I'll get rid of those red sheets on the bed at home.'

He was teasing her and she flushed delightfully, remembering what she had said that morning.

'I'll marry you whenever you like, and . . . and I rather like those sheets,' she answered shyly, still hardly able to believe that he loved her, making him laugh.

'We'll go round the world on this boat for our honeymoon,' he said gently, 'and never come back.'

China smiled at his echoing of her words. She could not imagine a nicer honeymoon.

She lifted her arms around his neck, secure in his love at last.

'Can we start now, will you make love to me?' she murmured achingly against his mouth, her fingers unbuttoning his shirt to find the warm hair-roughened skin of his chest. .

Ben drew a long hard breath as she caressed him.

'China. . . .' he began huskily, but she stopped him with her mouth, and as his powerful arms tightened around her, she knew that he could not resist her, that she had come home for ever.

Readers rave about Harlequin romance fiction...

"I absolutely adore Harlequin romances!
They are fun and relaxing to read, and
each book provides a wonderful escape."
— N.E.,* Pacific Palisades, California

"Harlequin is the best in romantic reading."
— K.G., Philadelphia, Pennsylvania

"Harlequin romances give me a whole new
outlook on life."
— S.P., Mecosta, Michigan_

"My praise for the warmth and adventure
your books bring into my life."
— D.F., Hicksville, New York

*Names available on request.

The bestselling epic saga of the Irish. An intriguing and passionate story that spans 400 years.

FIRST...
The Defiant

Lady Elizabeth Hatton, highborn Englishwoman, was not above using her position to get what she wanted ...and more than anything in the world she wanted Rory O'Donnell, the fiery Irish rebel. But it was an alliance that promised only ruin....

THEN...
The Survivors

Against a turbulent background of political intrigue and royal corruption, the determined, passionate Shanna O'Hara searched for peace in her beloved but troubled Ireland. Meanwhile in England, hot-tempered Brenna Coke fought against a loveless marriage....